# Escape of the Bridegroom

# Escape of the Bridegroom

# Chapter One

In the library of Wolverton Hall, time stood still.

Aidan, the ninth Baron Wolf, stared at his younger brother with the curious sensation that life was now forever divided into before this moment and after—if they were not to remain forever in this silent bubble of doom.

But, no, clearly, Aidan had misheard. He forced his eyes to blink, his lips to move. "Must give the old ears a clean. I thought you said your debts of honour amount to ten thousand pounds."

Patrick, standing rigid and white in front of the empty fireplace, said hoarsely, "I'm afraid it is so. I'm sorry, Aidan."

Slowly, Aidan sank into the armchair he had been about to sit in before Patrick blurted out his "difficulty."

"Sorry," Aidan repeated. The word didn't seem to have any meaning. "I don't *have* ten thousand or anything like it. We're done for."

Patrick tugged hard at his hair, then threw himself into the chair opposite. "I can't explain it, let alone excuse it. I was unforgivably stupid, because I began by winning a considerable amount which let me play deep for a change..."

"And let you lose all the quicker."

"Exactly."

For an instant, Patrick actually sounded pleased by his brother's understanding, so Aidan spelled out the rest, which they had both grown up knowing.

"There is no money. There is never any money. Everything that is not entailed is already mortgaged to the hilt or sold. Even selling the few remaining horses wouldn't bring anything like enough. It's not the sort of sum we can hope to borrow from friends. We're rolled up. Unless…" A faint flicker of hope struggled. "I suppose the play was fair?"

"Oh yes," Patrick said gloomily. "We were at White's."

"Of course you were."

"The devil's in it," Patrick agreed. "But the situation might not be impossible. There may be a way to borrow it."

Aidan groaned. "The moneylenders all know me. I used them when I was younger than you and nearly ruined the estate paying them off. They won't touch us."

"I know, I asked them already," Patrick admitted. "I didn't want to come to you with this but I can't fix it on my own."

"Can't fix it at all, Patrick." Like his brother, Aidan was a sociable man, of a happy-go-lucky nature. But he was not extravagant. He enjoyed life in the country among old friends, with occasional sorties to town. He had always stayed just about afloat, and had even begun to implement some new improvements to the land that should yield a little more. A drop in the ocean now.

One *had* to pay debts of honour. They would have to try to spread it over many years, which would affect everything and everyone, not least their own people, whether tenants, servants, family dependents….

"Whom do you owe?" Aidan asked, with a last fading hope.

Patrick closed his eyes. "Wilsborough. Graves, and Manning. Plus a few hundred to Dale."

"Well, Dale probably won't dun us, but the rest…" Aidan shuddered. "Are they still in Town? I'll go up tomorrow, see what I can negotiate with them."

"You'll hate that," Patrick said hoarsely. "*I* hate it. I'd give anything to undo that night but I can't. Even shooting myself would only land you with the debt instead. But the thing is, I *have* found a way out. Dale told me about it."

"About what?"

"About this cit. Romilly. Rich as Croesus and common as muck. He's been known to lend to the odd indigent gentleman in return for favours—the use of a name in his business, a word in Parliament, that kind of thing."

"I doubt he'd lend us ten thousand for *my* influence in Parliament," Aidan said dryly.

"You'd be surprised. He's so full of juice he doesn't know what to do with it all."

"Well, I'll drop in and make a suggestion," Aidan said sarcastically.

"I'm serious. He was pleased enough to see me when I tried—most amiable fellow you could meet. Thing is, he's got everything he could ever want, except acceptance into the upper echelons of society, because you can't buy that. For a few introductions and invitations, I believe he'd lend the money at very reasonable interest."

Aidan stared at him. "Seriously?"

"Oh yes, he couldn't quite bring himself to do it for me. I'm a younger son, untitled, but you're a baron, peer of the realm and all that."

"So he'd hand me ten thousand just for inviting him to dinner?"

"You probably wouldn't even need to have *him*. He knows he stinks of the shop. But he's got daughters, beautiful, educated, well-mannered daughters. They'd brighten any party if only people invited them. People like you, Aidan. Any number of hostesses would be happy to invite the Misses Romilly just to please you. Susanna would do it too. And no one would regret it."

"Wait a minute," Aidan said, blinking away the vision of his sister Susanna's face when asked to invite a couple of vulgar, over-dressed nobodies to her select parties. "How do you know these girls are such paragons? Not saying I care. For ten thousand pounds I'd introduce a beggar's ugly offspring to Lady Jersey."

Patrick was blushing. "Well, I've met them. The younger one, Miss Miranda Romilly, is *quite* out of the ordinary. Encountered her at Vauxhall and courted her favours, to tell the truth."

"You should know better," Aidan said austerely. "That sort will get you in trouble and straight into parson's mousetrap. Stick to opera dancers and women of our own class who understand the game."

"Yes, yes, and I was in no position to set her up anyway, even before I lost the ten thousand. But after Dale told me about her father, I did go and call on them, had a pleasant chat with Romilly himself. He was impressed. I may not be a rich man, but I do know everyone who is anyone amongst the ton."

"Not when you don't pay your debts of honour you won't," Aidan said flatly.

Patrick sighed. "I daresay he's aware of that. Still, thanks to Miranda, he did me the courtesy of listening, and though he declined to lend me the money, he did suggest he would be open to a visit from *you*. You being head of the family, and a baron."

Aidan shook his head, frowning. "It can't be as simple as that."

"Well, he must be a hard-headed man to have gathered all those pots of spare money," Patrick allowed. "I daresay he'll wring a lot of promises out of you that you'll be obliged to stir yourself to keep. Obviously, I'll help where I can. But it must be worth a try, Aidan. Only think of the humiliation of negotiating with the likes of Wilsborough and Graves."

Who were unlikely to budge an inch. Still...

"I don't believe in fairy godmothers," Aidan said bleakly. But when it came down to it, did he really have any choice?

HE WENT UP TO LONDON the following morning, traveling on the mail coach from Great Wolverton and arriving at the Wheel Inn in London in time for dinner. He took a room there and immediately composed a note to Mr. Romilly at the address Patrick had provided, stating that he would do himself the honour of calling at Mr. Romilly's abode at ten the following morning. Should this not be convenient, a note to that effect could reach him at the Wheel.

A boy was sent with his message, leaving Aidan with too much time to think.

If life was really as simple as walking up to a complete stranger and asking him to hand over ten thousand pounds in return for persuading a hostess of the ton to invite his daughters to a party... No, it was nonsense. Patrick must have got the wrong end of the stick, clutching at straws because of his own guilt.

A guilt he undoubtedly bore. Aidan should have annihilated him verbally, if not thrashed him too. To have got into such a state that he owed a sum of money he must have known he could never pay back... to have dropped it all on Aidan's shoulders, making a nonsense of everything he was trying to do...

The trouble was, Aidan had not really been trying to behave responsibly for very long himself. He had his youthful moments of folly, if not on quite such a grand scale. The Wolf estates had been teetering on the brink of bankruptcy for generations and the fact had never truly troubled Aidan. He muddled through, riding his luck, borrowing from friends when he had to, paying it back as soon as he could, juggling tradesmen's bills, occasionally robbing Peter to pay Paul, as the saying went, but never truly reneging on any debts. And no one could say he did not enjoy life. Much like Patrick.

He had also felt too numb yesterday to punish his brother as he fully deserved. It struck Aidan now, over dinner at the inn, that if by some miracle Romilly parted with the cash, it would be too easy, that it would teach Patrick nothing except that he could carry on doing exactly as he liked and something would always turn up to solve his problems. Aidan's grip on the purse strings would have to tighten. Patrick would have to find some way to earn his own money or at least stop spending it.

But there was no point in even considering such ideas. Aidan did not believe in miracles or in saintly cits. He knew in his heart he would be going from Romilly's house to Wilsborough's. And the rest.

He tugged at his cravat, which felt too tight and hot and uncomfortable.

*Bloody Patrick, I will never forgive you for this...*

Better for Patrick probably if he never did. Only he knew he would. He only had one brother.

After a restless night and too little sleep, Aidan broke his fast and walked to Russell Square, off which resided Mr. Romilly and his family.

A liveried footman opened the door to his knock, took his card, and without any fuss, led him straight upstairs to Mr. Romilly's study.

This was a pleasant apartment overlooking the square, light and bright, with comfortable furnishings that were yet just a shade too opulent for good taste. A small man—presumably Romilly himself—rose from behind his large, highly-polished desk, beaming with apparent pleasure.

He bowed low. "My Lord Wolf. I am honoured to meet you at last."

"Mr. Romilly," Aidan said coolly, inclining his head. "Thank you for receiving me."

"How could I not? It is not every day we welcome the aristocracy to our humble abode. Besides, I have the pleasure of Mr. Patrick Wolf's acquaintance, so I almost feel we are old friends."

Romilly spoke with a distinctly plebian accent, a rather odd mixture of northern England and London's east end. But although he made no effort to disguise his speech, he wore an expensively tailored coat and he smelled not of the shop but of the finest sandalwood soap.

Aidan, who was never high in the instep, would have been happy enough, despite his embarrassment, to shake hands with the man, but

Romilly clearly felt it would have been presumptuous to offer. Instead, he indicated the well upholstered chair at the opposite side of the desk.

"Please, sit down, my lord. A small sherry perhaps? Or a brandy?"

"Thank you, no." Aidan sat down.

"Then you will allow me to ring for tea."

"Not on my account, sir," Aidan said firmly. "Though I beg you will feel free on your own."

"Well, I'm convinced too much tea rots a man from the inside out," Romilly said cheerfully, and at last resumed his chair. "How is young Mr. Wolf?"

"In excellent health when I left him yesterday at Wolverton Hall." There was no point in beating about the bush, and Aidan wanted the matter dealt with so that he would know how much crawling he was going to have to do with Wilsborough and the rest. "Although he is rightly and thoroughly ashamed of himself. He tells me he acquainted you with his...trouble."

"His trouble which inevitably has become yours," Romilly said sympathetically.

"Indeed. I shall come to the point, sir. I am in need of a loan to pay my brother's debts. The estate cannot support it, as I am sure you know, and yet my brother seems to think that you might be willing to help us."

Romilly beamed. "I am a tradesman, my lord. I know you gentlemen don't like to hear it, but we are all traders at heart, whether we are trading cotton, wheat, money, horses, or favours. I have plenty of what you currently need most, and I am sure you have something that I need. There is always a deal—a trade, indeed—to be made."

"I have nothing to secure a loan upon," Aidan said bluntly. "My property is all entailed or already mortgaged. As I presume my brother told you, he needs ten thousand pounds. I cannot ask you for such a sum without security, but if you will lend a portion of it over a long period, I might be able to negotiate the rest with the gentlemen concerned. I should be obliged if you would tell me at once. Is it something you might consider, or am I wasting your time and my own?"

Romilly smiled again. "I do not consider my time wasted, sir, and I hope, neither will you. I am in a position to lend you the full ten thousand—or even double that to help bring your estates into order—without any interest at all, in return for certain favours that will benefit my family."

Aidan gazed at him, at first unable to believe his ears. And then, dangerously, he began to hope.

Squashing that hope, he said honestly, "I cannot imagine any favour in my power to bestow is worth ten, let alone twenty, thousand pounds."

"Ah, well that is because you are not looking at things from my position. I am a humble man by birth, Lord Wolf. I might have made a great deal of money, but that will never buy me respectability, nor the best society for my daughters and grandchildren. In short, I have gone as far in life as I can go without you. As you, it seems, have gone as far as you can without me."

"It is a generous way to look on the matter," Aidan said ruefully. "What exactly is it you would want me to do for you?"

"Introduce my daughters to the ton."

Dear God, was Patrick right and it was really going to be so simple? If so, why had no one bitten the man's hand off before for such sums?

He swallowed. "I am not married, sir, so my efforts would be limited. But my sister, Lady Bryton, would be happy to invite them to her house for an extended party next month. Other invitations might well stem from that. And come the spring and the Season, I am acquainted with several hostesses who would be glad to invite the Misses Romilly. Once set on that road, I am sure your daughters will take Society by storm. From what my brother tells me, they are diamonds of the first water."

Romilly preened unashamedly. "Miranda is a beauty. Eve, not so much, though she has qualities a discerning man would value even more. They were educated at Mrs. Elphinstone's Academy for Young Ladies at Queen's Square and will disgrace no one by their manners. Unlike their papa who is too old to change."

"And that is all you want of me?" Aidan said, still disbelieving.

"*All*? It may seem little to your lordship, but it means a great deal to *me* that you are prepared to do your best for my girls. Can you promise me that much?"

"To do my best for them?" Aidan repeated, hope catching at his very breath. "And for you, sir?"

Romilly laughed. "Oh, I can see to my own affairs, my lord, but I cannot step out of my class. Now, I know a gentleman's word is his bond, but being no gentleman myself, we'll have it all written down and signed, nice and legal, and you may draw on my bank this very day. Now, are we agreed on twenty thousand?"

Aidan blinked. "No, sir, we are not. I'll never pay off such a sum. Let us agree on the ten I requested."

"As you wish," Romilly said, drawing paper toward himself. "Let me just pour us a drink to celebrate our understanding..." He rose and poured brandy into two glasses. Presenting one to Aidan, he clinked it with his own. "To our new partnership."

Numb with incredible relief, Aidan sipped, welcoming the burn of the liquid as a sign of life and reality.

As Romilly sat back down and began to write busily, Aidan watched him.

"That is all you want of me in return?" he said anxiously.

"Your best efforts for my daughters," Romilly repeated distractedly, his pen still flying across the page as though he did not even have to think about the wording.

"Don't you want to involve a solicitor?" Aidan said, with sudden shame at taking such advantage of the man.

"Damned leeches," Romilly said mildly. "I've learned enough over the years to do without them now. For the most part. So, just ten thousand? Are you sure? It will make no difference to your side of the bargain. I shall not charge you interest."

Aidan swallowed. "Call it twelve and I can make some necessary repairs on the estate."

"Then shall we say over fifteen years? With extensions guaranteed for years of drought and bad harvest."

"Very generous of you," Aidan said sincerely.

"I really do want the best for my girls."

"Very commendable of you. I wish I had done more to keep my brother in line. And myself!"

"Tush." Romilly glanced up, his eyes twinkling. "If you had been so perfect, we would never have met."

Aidan sipped his brandy, imagining Wilsborough's face when he threw the money in his lap; planning the lecture he would read to Patrick and the promises they would both make to change their lives with this gift that was falling into their laps...

Aidan still felt bemused by the time Romilly pushed two sheets of paper across the desk to him.

"If you're happy, we'll have my clerk in to witness our signatures," Romilly said. "There are two copies there, one for each of us, exactly the same. It binds each of us to what we have agreed. In the event that I break our bargain, you owe me nothing. In the event that you do, you must pay me all the money back. Is that fair?"

"Well, yes, except that you know I could not pay."

"It will be a large debt," Romilly agreed, "and in the event of it occurring, there would be interest. But there, we are men of our word, and you will not renege on doing your best for my daughters."

How hard could it be?

Aidan read the document, which echoed so exactly the words Romilly had actually spoken, that he soon merely skimmed it, picking up the most important phrases.

*Lord Wolf promises, to the best of his ability, to introduce Mr. Romilly's daughters, Miss Eve Romilly and Miss Miranda Romilly, to his friends in Society and to otherwise promote their social standing to the best of his ability, as discussed and defined in this agreement...*

*Mr. Romilly agrees to give to Lord Wolf the sum of twelve thousand pounds to be repaid annually over fifteen years... except in the event of bad harvests when a further year will be added to the term of the loan...*

*Said twelve thousand pounds will be paid this day, the second of August 1813, to Lord Wolf...*

"Well?" Romilly asked.

A small, fading voice in Aidan's brain whispered still that this was too good to be true. But he was desperate, and God knew if he had to dance attendance on these females for entire Seasons, it would still be better than social and financial ruin.

Aidan met Romilly's gaze. "I am getting the best of this bargain."

"You are. But I believe we are in agreement?"

Aidan drew in his breath. "We are."

Romilly beamed. "Then let's have Henley in and sign, and we'll get the money to you."

He tugged the bell behind him and a gangly, balding man entered almost at once from a connecting door and bowed low to each of them. Solemnly, both Romilly and Aidan signed both copies of their agreement, and Mr. Henley the clerk signed as witness, and departed.

Romilly folded both documents, passed one to Aidan and placed his own in the drawer of his desk. Then he reached for the brandy decanter to refill their glasses.

"I expect you would like to meet my Eve before we drink to your happiness," Romilly said, tugging a different bell rope by the fireplace.

Aidan, who was more eager to get his hands on the money, remembered his part of the bargain and said civilly. "I shall of course be happy to meet both your daughters."

"Miranda is out, sadly. She will be upset to miss the first announcement of her sister's engagement."

Aidan blinked. "Engagement?"

"Send Miss Eve to us," Romilly instructed the footman who had appeared at the door. And to Aidan: "Betrothal, if you prefer. What could be better for my daughters than the marriage of one of them to a baron? But you have a wonderful bargain, my lord! Eve will make an excellent Lady Wolf. If you apply for the special license today, I daresay you can be married within the week."

Deliberately, Aidan set his glass down upon the desk. "I did not promise marriage."

"Oh but you did," Romilly said, smiling. "It is there in the small letters at the bottom of the page, defining your *best* and our agreed efforts to promote the social status of my daughters. Making one of them Lady Wolf would, after all, be your very best effort on their behalf."

# Chapter Two

Eve Romilly had been with her father when she had first seen Lord Wolf striding down the road toward their house. Her heart had never before skipped a beat at the sight of a man, but this gentleman was quite out of the ordinary. It had nothing to do with expensive tailoring or a confident swagger—in fact, his clothes, although correct and well-fitting morning dress, looked a trifle old and he walked with purpose, his movements quick and unstudied. But it was his face that caught her attention.

He was, simply, the most handsome man she had ever seen, his features dark and yet refined, his mouth firm and shapely. A serious man, with an unconscious frown of worry. And yet it was not, she thought, a face without humour or intelligence. A good man who liked to laugh. More than that, a man who liked to *live*. Vitality seemed to blaze out of his eyes, out of every swift step and swing of his long, slender body.

Although not given to fantasies, she thought she would like this man, even without that rare little tug of pure, physical attraction.

At first, she had not connected him with her father's scheming, for Papa was happily gloating about something to do with Miranda and her chief new admirer, the charming if indigent Mr. Patrick Wolf.

"Mark my words," he was saying, "my grandchildren will be lords and ladies yet."

"I really doubt it is marriage Mr. Wolf has in mind," Eve murmured a little dreamily for her attention was still on the stranger in the street below. "You should warn Miranda, Papa, for she does not listen to me and my aunt encourages her in—"

"*That* is our man," Papa interrupted with glee. "And quite unfashionably punctual. That my dear, is one desperate baron. Run along now until I send for you. Change your dress, though, for you're much too frumpy."

"But Papa, I was going with Mr. Neville to—"

"Not today. I want you here. If all goes well, I'll send for you in one hour and I'll expect you to be well dressed and on your best behaviour. No dreary chatter about orphans, no cutting comments or criticism of the idle rich. For once, take a leaf out of your sister's book. At least she understands gentlemen."

It was on the tip of Eve's tongue to point out that Miranda clearly did not understand gentlemen if she imagined Patrick Wolf contemplated marriage with her, but her father was clearly not interested, shooing her from the room into the connecting office of his clerk, Mr. Henley, and firmly closing the door.

The knowledge that Papa was about to receive the beautiful man in the adjoining room made her stomach tingle.

"Mr. Henley," she whispered. "Who is my father's visitor?"

"Lord Wolf, miss."

"Oh dear..." She paused in her rush toward the door to the landing. Foolishly, she had wanted a closer look at the stranger—without being disloyal to Mr. Neville, of course—but clearly the man had come to detach his brother from Miranda's clutches. Surely Papa could not be so mistaken as to believe his visitor wished to discuss marriage contracts?

Papa was rarely mistaken, of course, but in his obsession with aristocratic grandchildren, his judgement was seriously impaired. She waited until she heard the footman announce the visitor and retreat back downstairs before she fled to make her own arrangements.

First, she had to scribble a quick apology to Mr. Neville for failing to accompany him to the orphanage. She was annoyed, for she had been looking forward to the visit—she liked the children and God knew they needed a few outings away from the bleak, leaky building which currently housed them. She was helping Mr. Neville raise funds for a larger, better home for them, but donations were slow.

She sent Georgie the boot boy—himself a former resident of the orphanage—scampering off to the vicarage with her note, put an end to a squabble between the housemaid and the kitchen maid, and went upstairs to her own bedchamber to change.

What did Papa expect of her? As she raked through her gowns without enthusiasm, the reason for her father's ebullience suddenly struck her.

He was no fool, and he saw the Wolf brothers as his means to acquiring aristocratic grandchildren. Therefore, he had some means of compelling the marriage.

She dropped her hands back to her sides, frowning. Did Miranda know about this? Had she gone off with their aunt to buy new gowns in which to celebrate her betrothal to a baron's heir? Did she not realize how resentful her husband would be of such a compulsion? In any case, from Eve's glimpse of the baron, he was hardly likely to oblige Papa by dying any time soon. It could be decades before Miranda became Lady Wolf.

She *would* move in the first circles, though, and she would like that. Until she realized she was despised by those she imagined were her friends, and by her husband. Eve shuddered at the prospect of such misery and humiliation.

In truth, she was weary of all these schemes. Papa was never happy unless he was plotting, and Miranda seemed to have inherited the trait. Eve, on the other hand, longed for a quiet life, doing something worthwhile in the company of a good and gentle man.

Mr. Neville did not make her heart flutter. He was older, more thoughtful than she imagined the baron to be, and ambitious only for the spiritual wellbeing of his parishioners and the physical care of the orphans. It was good work, but Papa was not yet ready to consider Mr.

Neville as a son-in-law. Perhaps with Miranda safely married to Patrick Wolf

Only, Miranda's unhappiness would be unbearable.

Eve sat down on her bed to think. She knew she was guilty of assuming everyone felt as she did, and in fact this was rarely true of Miranda. The mischievous child had grown into an ambitious, self-obsessed young woman, more attuned to her father's thoughts than to Eve's.

Miranda wanted this marriage. And who was Eve to try and take it from her? Miranda laughed at Mr. Neville.

"Even *you* could do better than him!"

Eve did not like conflict. She did not wish to quarrel with her father or her sister. But at the same time, she had no intention of letting them stand in her way. When the time was right, she *would* marry Mr. Neville, with or without their approval. She had to allow her sister the same choice.

Not that she could stop her. Their father was behind Miranda's marriage.

So why was Miranda allowed to go out with their aunt this morning, while Eve was kept at home?

To show Lord Wolf the respectability of the family? It had to be that, for Miranda was more beautiful and much more charming to parade before the baron.

Sighing, Eve went again to the wardrobe and took out the blue morning gown. It was this season's, though plain like most of her clothes, but it was definitely ladylike, cool and respectable. That was the part she must play to convince the baron that his brother's marriage into the family would be acceptable.

She just hoped it was the right thing to do because part of her wanted to behave like a harpy, bedecked in jewels and silks that were too small for her, just to put Lord Wolf off. Wouldn't they all be happier that way?

No. She firmly believed that everyone should have the right and the responsibility to choose their own path through life. Therefore, she would play the obedient daughter one more time; and tomorrow she would speak again to Mr. Neville and tell her father she was going to be married.

Her mind made up, she rang for the lady's maid she shared with Miranda.

Her father sent for her while the maid was still dressing her hair in one of Miranda's ridiculously elaborate styles.

"Never mind," Eve said, brushing the dismayed girl's hands away. Dragging her fingers through her hair, she sent pins flying in all directions. In a couple of seconds, she had seized the rope of her hair, wound it tight into a simple knot at the back of her head, and stabbed in a few pins to hold it. "It's respectable," she told the maid, and marched out to play her part.

Her father's voice was at its most jovial as he answered her knock, so when she walked into his study, she was utterly unprepared for the tension that froze her in her tracks.

Her father stood in the middle of the room, beaming with triumph and good humour, a brandy glass held in his short, stubby fingers. "Eve, my dearest, come in and make your curtsey to Lord Wolf."

Obediently, Eve curtseyed in the general direction of the unmoving figure in the chair by the desk. Only as she straightened, raising her eyes to his face at last, she almost staggered backward under the blast of fury and contempt blazing in his face.

Stunned, since she had done nothing to deserve such hatred, she cast a pleading glance at her father for guidance.

Lord Wolf finally rose to his feet—which, by all the rules of courtesy, he should have done the moment she entered the room.

Dear God, she had been wrong when she imagined him good-humoured and a little anxious. He was all ice and steel and loathing.

*Oh, Papa, what have you done?*

"Allow me to be the first to congratulate you, my darling," her father said, embracing her. "I have just received his lordship's most flattering offer for your hand in marriage, and I'm delighted to say I have accepted."

Eve's jaw dropped. Her father stepped back and she gazed at him, uncomprehending. Someone in the room appeared to be mad.

Papa was not looking at her but at the baron. "Is that not correct, my lord?"

Lord Wolf didn't look at her either. His gaze was locked with her father's, his eyes hard as agates, his face dripping with all the haughty contempt of the aristocrat for the presuming, vulgar mushroom.

But she had no time either to cringe in shame or defend her family.

"Quite correct," Lord Wolf drawled. "Providing I get my money."

It was so deliberately insulting that heat burned up her face with bewilderment and anger. He plucked something off the desk—it looked like a banker's draft—and strolled toward the door. "Arrangements may be made by letter. Good morning."

He did not trouble to close the door. It was Eve who did that before turning her anxious gaze on her father, whose smile had slipped a little.

"What have you done?" she asked hoarsely.

The smile returned in full force. "I have arranged a marriage for you with Lord Wolf."

"But...but Miranda—"

"Don't be silly! I would not waste Miranda on a mere baron, let alone on his untitled brother. This is perfect. Because as Lady Wolf, you will introduce your sister to the ton. I daresay she will marry a duke in the end!"

"I daresay she will," Eve said tartly, "but it will be without my help. Papa, I respectfully decline his lordship's offer, since I am already engaged to marry Mr. Neville."

"The vicar fellow?" Her father gave a derisive chuckle. "Don't be silly, Eve. You will marry Wolf, for your family and his survival."

"Survival?" she repeated, distracted as he'd probably known she would be. "How is his survival threatened?"

Papa shrugged. "Well, financial and social survival, but you know these honourable types. I daresay he would rather shoot himself than become an outcast."

"Why on earth should he become an outcast? Particularly if he does not marry *me*!"

"Because he has taken on young Patrick's gambling debts. I know it makes no sense that such debts are considered honourable while the tailor's bill may be ignored until the poor tailor is bankrupted, but that's the Quality for you."

Eve stared at him, but she had never been slow. "You sold me for the price of Patrick's gambling debts?"

"Don't be offended! They amount to ten thousand pounds, plus another two to get his lordship's land in order."

"But...Papa, you can't do this! It is my life and I have plans with Mr. Neville—"

"Neville," her father said with contempt. "He's nearly as old as me. I've given you a younger, fitter, much more handsome man with a title—"

"And nothing but contempt for me and mine!" Eve interrupted. "Did you not see how he looked at me? At us? Papa, he is not someone you can manipulate with impunity!"

"I already have." Complaisance suffused his voice and his face. "You will be Lady Wolf within the week."

The blood drained from her face. "But I can't," she said, truly panicked now. "I won't!"

MIRANDA, OF COURSE, laughed like a drain when she heard. "How wonderful of you, Papa! I can't pretend I'm not a little bit miffed that Eve will be married before me, but he's only a baron after all, and once she's married to him, I shall have the pick of the ton."

Eve gave up. She should never have expected any sense let alone help from her sister. Abandoning Miranda and Papa in the drawing room, she seized her cloak and hat and went out into the rain in search of Mr. Neville.

She found him in the vicarage, drying out in his parlour after getting soaked during his return from the orphanage.

"Miss Romilly!" he exclaimed as she brushed past the housekeeper. "My dear lady, you should not be here unaccompanied!"

"But I'm desperate!" she exclaimed, throwing herself onto the hearth at his feet.

"Tea, Mrs. Pye," he said in alarm. He was a gentle, formal man, which was one reason why, despite their wish to marry, they were not yet on Christian name terms. The other reason was harder for her to fathom but had something to do with his being sixteen years her senior and the man she most respected in the world.

The door had barely shut on the housekeeper before Eve burst into tears. Somehow, she managed to pour out the whole tale of her father's infamy and his high-handed betrothal of her to an aristocratic stranger whom she was expected to marry within the week.

Kindly, if somewhat awkwardly, Mr. Neville patted her shoulder. Wiping her face as her story shuddered to a halt, Eve saw the sorrow in his eyes. It didn't comfort her.

"My dear, you owe your father obedience," he said hoarsely. "The laws of God and man agree on that."

"But my father compelled him—"

"That was very wrong of him. On the other hand, Mr. Romilly is helping him out of his financial difficulties and giving him a wife who is beyond price. I have cause to know that."

She stared at him. *You will not fight for me.*

"I – I thought you wanted to marry me," she said in a small, flat voice. Desolation washed over her.

"I do. The happiness you have brought me... The happiness I had hoped for... I cannot deny this pains me as much as it does you. But God moves in mysterious ways. Who are we to doubt Him? Perhaps this is how you can do most good."

"But he hates me!"

Mr. Neville took her hands in his. "Lord Wolf? He has been bested in a bargain. It upsets men. But if he is remotely human, he will soon realize the true treasure that is his wife. Through you, he and his brother might well mend their ways. And help our orphans besides."

Eve blinked. She was not a good enough person to have even considered their plight amidst her own crisis. "Help our orphans? I hardly think Lord Wolf is in a position to donate what we need."

"But he is," Mr. Neville said seriously. "The building I showed you last week—"

"The big, old house with the little park?" she said impatiently. "Just beyond Covent Garden? Basically sound but in need of repair."

"It belongs to Lord Wolf."

She sat up straight. "Then he could sell it to pay Patrick's debts! He's probably forgotten all about it!" And she wouldn't need to marry him at all...

"He might have forgotten, for it's clearly no use to him. But neither can he sell it. The solicitors explained it to me when I inquired. It's part of the entail on Lord Wolf's property."

"Oh." Her shoulders sagged again.

"Don't you see, dear Miss Romilly?" Mr. Neville's unworldly eyes were shining again. "You may be the instrument by which our orphans find their new home. With your dowry and your good influence, his lordship can surely make the necessary repairs and let the house to us for a very nominal rent. It would be perfect."

Everyone's life, it seemed, would be perfect, if only she made the sacrifice.

No, Mr. Neville would not fight for her. He would give her up for his orphans. It was not the kind of love she secretly craved. In fact, she had a sneaking suspicion he was secretly relieved by not having to alter his life to accommodate her.

Never had she felt so alone and friendless.

Her life was falling apart.

Mrs. Pye, who had been tactfully taking her time, now entered with the tea. Miserable with rejection, Eve rose, wiped her eyes once more and gave herself a severe talking-to. She might be plain and unlovable, but she was no milksop.

She could make the best of what had been decided without her.

Or she could run away.

OVER THE NEXT FEW DAYS, she flitted between the two choices before her. Running was the more appealing option. An adventure, far away from everyone who knew her, and she had her generous allowance, mostly saved, to make that a practical possibility, or at least a beginning.

And yet, stupidly, her father's honour as well as the Wolf brothers' ruin depended on her staying.

She did not see his lordship again to help convince her one way or the other. The two images of him that she held in her mind—the most handsome, appealing man she had ever seen in the street below the window, versus the most implacable and frightening enemy when she finally met him in the study—began to blur.

Marriage with Mr. Neville would never now happen, so it might as well be Wolf as anyone else. Maybe she could make it work somehow to the orphans' benefit if to no one else's. At least it would get her out of this house of schemes and tantrums. Only, she wasn't sure she could bear his lordship's contempt as she bore her family's. His hatred shrivelled her heart even as it angered her mind. He considered her the price of his ten thousand pounds. He would marry her for his brother's sake and there would be no pretence of anything else. He meant her and her father both to know how much he despised them for it.

A stupid, entitled man who could not or would not see that it was himself and his brother he should despise for creating this situation. Not the man who had offered him the way out. And certainly not the woman who was their sacrificial pawn.

*Run, Evie, run...*

While she vacillated, packing and then unpacking her light travelling bag several times, a few letters were exchanged between her father and Lord Wolf. Apparently, none of them mentioned her.

And then, on the fourth morning after the catastrophic visit, she was dragged out of bed by Miranda and their aunt, and informed that today was her wedding day. Exhausted and bewildered after several nights of very little sleep, she found herself splashed with cold water and crammed, shivering, into her least favourite gown. They primped her hair and scented her skin, giggling and chattering until her head hurt and her spirit crumpled.

Even that she could have borne if her bridegroom had only once looked at her as she walked across the drawing room, trembling on her father's arm. But he didn't.

And then came the unkindest cut of all.

Mr. Neville, dignified and sad-eyed, stepped forward to perform the ceremony.

It was too late to run. But not too late for tears.

# Chapter Three

Aidan, who was good-natured at heart, had never before maintained this level of fury for so long. Part of it was certainly aimed at Patrick for getting him into this mess, but most of it was reserved for Romilly.

Marrying for money had a long and shameful tradition amongst the aristocracy. And on his more realistic days, Aidan was aware it was what he would have to do one day. One distant day, not now, not by trickery, and not when he had no say in his choice of bride.

None of his anger was for *her*. He barely considered her at all. His one glimpse of her had shown him a tall, slender, young woman in a plain blue dress, with a plain, severe face. Not even the pretty one Patrick had told him about. But in truth, he hardly noticed her features, for he didn't care what she looked like. He had no intention of spending any time with her before he absolutely had to.

So, with his brother's debts of honour fully paid and a healthy two thousand pounds sitting in his bank, he stalked into Romilly's house to marry Romilly's daughter. He wore the same clothes as he had on his previous visit and acknowledged the others in the room with the stiffest of bows—Romilly himself, an aunt, an uncle, an anaemic clergyman with stooped shoulders, and the beautiful sister once pursued by Patrick with dishonourable intent.

The aunt chattered in an excited sort of a way and snivelled when Romilly strode to meet the bride, presumably, at the drawing room door.

Aidan stared straight ahead. The clergyman stepped in front of him and Romilly, still beaming—how Aidan longed to smack that smile off his smug lips—placed the bride's trembling hand on his.

Savagely, Aidan wondered if she shook with excitement at reaching the dizzying rank of baroness, or with fear of placing herself in the power of an angry and resentful husband. His lips curled into a sneer, and he actually cast her a curious glance.

Neither excitement nor fear, then. Tears stood out in her eyes. One even trembled on a long, dark eyelash.

Shocked, he turned his attention to the clergyman, who had begun the words of the ceremony that would bind him for life to this weeping girl. For the first time, he considered her part in this. She knew him no more than he knew her. Who or what was she was so sad to be leaving behind?

Well, she should have thought of that before. With a resurgence of anger, his brief instant of concern evaporated. If he had sold himself for the price of his brother's debts, she had sold herself to be a peeress. Her tears merely hardened his resolve to be done with this, and with her, as quickly as possible.

He uttered the responses required tonelessly. So did she. He placed the plain gold ring on her finger. At least she had a lady's hands, soft and slender, but then she must have grown up considerably more pampered than he.

The clergyman's voice cracked slightly as he pronounced them man and wife, and then he turned away to allow Romilly and his family to embrace the bride.

Aidan found his hand pumped by the uncle and Romilly himself.

The beautiful sister gave him her hand most prettily. "Congratulations, my lord. We are all disappointed not to see Mr. Wolf by your side this morning."

"He is at Wolverton Hall, where we shall repair as soon as Lady Wolf is ready."

"I'm ready now," said the new Lady Wolf flatly. "My bag is already packed. My family will see the rest of my things sent on."

"Of course we shall, dearest," the aunt promised. "But you must eat first!"

"Sadly, we have not the time if we are to reach Wolverton Hall by nightfall," said Aidan. "The post-chaise will be here directly."

That, he was glad to see, caused a few smiles to wobble, and cast something of a blight over their triumph. It even caused Romilly to take him aside with the first hint of anxiety he had ever betrayed.

"You will remember our agreement," Romilly said. "Your part of the bargain does not end with the wedding."

"I am quite as aware as you of our agreement," Aidan said, and was delighted to see the unease cross his father-in-law's face. "And like you, I shall keep it to the letter."

The drawing room door opened, and an elderly butler announced that a post-chaise and four was at the front door for Lord and Lady Wolf.

To Aidan's surprise, his bride sailed straight out of the door without so much as a glance at any of her family. Aidan spared them a distant bow and a "Good morning," and then he followed his wife out of the house and into the carriage where she already sat, upright and silent. She did not wave to her rather desperately smiling family at the door.

Either she now considered herself far above them. Or she was no happier about the marriage than he was. Which was at least interesting.

And at least she wasn't crying.

The postilions set the horses in motion. The outriders kept pace. Aidan knew a brief urge to swap with one of them rather than spend hours alone with the wife he did not want.

He regarded her broodingly from the back-facing seat while she gazed blindly out of the window. She was not actually plain, he discovered with some surprise. Although her features were a little sharp, the severity he had vaguely noticed in her face was softened by a more forgiving hairstyle and the unexpectedly dashing bonnet perched upon her curls. But her expression was still rigid, like her thin, upright body.

She shifted restlessly. "How long is the journey, my lord?"

"With decent horses, about eight hours or so. Don't feel obliged to stay awake and make conversation with me."

"I don't. But I would like to know what is ahead of me."

"A draughty old house in need of repair," he said with some satisfaction.

"You needn't labour the point sir. Let us take it as read that you would not have married me were you not in dire financial straits. Who will I find there, and what do you expect of me?"

"I expect nothing of you," he said at once. "We have few servants. My brother is currently at home. I believe you are acquainted with him."

"I met him twice when he called for Miranda. And your expectations?"

He caught her quick, surreptitious glance and held it with malicious amusement. "You refer to the marriage bed?"

Her face flamed. "I do not."

He spoke through her. "You need have no fears on that score. Or at least not yet. I already have what I require of you. At some point, I shall need an heir, but happily, that should not be urgent for several years."

He was aware as he said the words, that they were unnecessarily offensive, and yet he could not stop them. He didn't even want to, for he was still angry. But her glance of contempt took him by surprise.

"I believe a gentleman would take that as read, too."

A flash of shame heated his face, though he retorted. "I thought you wished to know what was ahead of you. The answer, of course, is whatever you wish. You hold the purse strings and you are mistress of Wolverton Hall. You are at liberty to arrange things however you wish. I ask only that you leave my own private rooms undisturbed without consulting me."

"I shall disturb you as little as possible."

The words might have been meek, but he was not deaf to the fervour of her tone. His lips twitched without his permission, but at least she did not appear to notice. Her attention was once more on the window view.

"Is your household aware of our approach?" she asked with studied indifference.

"My letter to that effect should have reached them yesterday. Your apartments should be ready to receive you."

She nodded once and closed her eyes.

He felt dismissed, which for some reason did not please him. He had been assuming the high ground in this disastrous marriage, but it struck him that he was losing it by giving in to temper. He had made his bed and had best learn to lie in it.

As the hours and the miles flew past, mostly in silence as she kept her eyes closed, his natural optimism began at last to reassert itself.

Patrick's debt was paid and the price of it should at least have taught him a lesson. Aidan had two thousand pounds to spend on what was most necessary.

Romilly had reminded him of their agreement. There was no need, but Aidan did not consider there was any rush in such matters. He had the money and the wife, and now he was quite prepared to stretch as far as he could the rest of the agreement he had been tricked into signing. It would serve Romilly right.

The spring was quite time enough to introduce the new Lady Wolf and her sister to society. Until then, he saw no need to change his life one jot. And even in the spring, he would do the bare minimum. After all, by marrying her, he had already given his best.

"YOU MUST TELL ME," he said as the horses were changed for the third time, "when you wish to stop for refreshment."

"Perhaps at the next change," she said, and closed her eyes once more.

Aidan was relieved. He should not have dismissed the wedding breakfast out of hand although it had given him a certain amount of satisfaction at the time, for by now his stomach was rumbling.

At the next inn, they alighted while the horses were changed. They were served a meal in the common room. Aidan ate heartily. His wife merely picked at her plate.

"Not what you're used to?" he asked with no pretence at sympathy.

"I am not hungry. Merely thirsty."

Ten minutes later, they were back in the carriage and speeding on to Wolverton Hall. Aidan longed for the journey to end. He wanted to be away from his wife. She clearly wanted to be away from him.

But their arrival turned out to be even worse. The entire household had considered it appropriate to turn out to welcome his bride as mistress, thus revealing the embarrassing paucity of servants and the decrepitude of the Listons, the couple in charge as butler and housekeeper respectively.

Patrick, managing to look appallingly guilty and jovial at the same time, bounced down the front steps to greet them. He kissed the bride's hand and cheek—which was more than Aidan had ever done—and embraced his brother rather too tightly.

"I'm so sorry, Aidan, I didn't mean you to make a sacrifice like this..." he muttered.

The new Lady Wolf sailed ahead, greeting Mrs. Liston as though she had been born to the role. As if she hadn't heard Patrick's unfortunate apology. Only Aidan was sure, somehow that she had heard. It was no worse than anything *he* had said quite deliberately to make her pay.

Although it was late, well after nine o'clock by the time they arrived, a light supper had been served in the dining room. His nerves were by then at screaming point, but Aidan felt obliged not to disappoint his anxious staff.

"We'll eat and then I'll show you to your rooms," he declared to his wife.

"I've dined already," Patrick said awkwardly. "Shall I leave you to it?"

"God, no," Aidan said, appalled.

And this time, it was his wife's lips that gave a faint twitch.

As if sensing his mood, Patrick took on the burden of conversation, aided civilly by his sister-in-law.

*Christ, do I even know her name? Miranda is the other one. Perhaps "my lady" will do in the circumstances...*

He thought back to the only half-heard wedding ceremony. *Eve. She's called Eve.*

The remembrance was an unexpected relief. But he was still heartily glad when the meal came to a close. Patrick effaced himself at once, and Aidan led his bride through the slightly dusty, discreetly empty passages to the traditional apartments of the baroness.

The rooms had been unoccupied since his mother's death in childbirth almost twenty years ago. The servants had done their best, airing the rooms, and lighting fires to take away the edge of cold and damp, and the bed had been made up with the best linen. Which still wasn't great. They were hardly welcoming apartments. The carpets and the hangings were old, some of them even moth-eaten, and the air smelled faintly musty. Aidan felt a twinge of guilt.

"You must do as you see fit with these rooms," he said abruptly. "Have them redecorated to your own taste. Likewise with the rest of the house."

"Apart from your own apartments. I do remember my instructions."

"Yes, well. Neither of us has had any time to prepare the practicalities. We must just make the best of it."

Was that relief softening her eyes? A faint smile, timid and yet eager, curved her lips which were suddenly not severe at all, but curiously vulnerable and almost pretty.

"I will, my lord. We need not hate each other."

"I don't hate you," he said in surprise.

Her eyes were serious, perceptive. "But you are angry."

"Not with you," he said ruefully. "I apologize for giving such an impression. It is your father who angers me."

"Why?" she asked. "You got your money and you agreed to the price."

"I was tricked into paying the price," he retorted.

She sat down on the bed as though trying out the mattress for comfort. In very different circumstance and several years hence, he had meant to bring his chosen bride to this bed...

"But I read the contract," she said, frowning. "There was no trick. I think you are angry at yourself for being so eager for the money that you did not read it carefully enough before you signed."

He stared at her. Alarm showed in her eyes, though she did not back down. And God knew there was more than an element of truth in her words. But he was damned if he'd admit it. His most pressing need was to get out of there with his dignity intact.

"I'll bid you goodnight," he said abruptly and strode out of the bedchamber into the equally unprepossessing sitting room. He was halfway across it before it struck him she had brought no servants with her.

He turned on his heel and hurried back into the bedroom, almost colliding with her in the doorway.

Instinctively, he caught her arm to steady her. She was so thin, he felt her bones, fragile like a bird's, and knew an unwelcome urge to protect this unwanted creature, who stared up at him now with wide, startled brown eyes.

Surprise robbed her of her armour of severity, and he saw her again as the vulnerable young girl who wept secretly as her hand had been placed in his. Whatever triumph Romilly got out of this wedding, it was not shared by his daughter.

For the first time, he was forced to consider the situation from her point of view. She could not have been much more than twenty years old, but she had the character to stand up to him. And the gentleness to feel every contemptuous barb he had thrown at her.

Even now, she did not step back from his unpalatable nearness, nor pull her arm free.

Instead of what he meant to say, he blurted, "You did not want this either. Was there someone else?"

She nodded once.

"Who?" he asked, both curious and pitying.

Her lips twitched unhappily. "The man who married us."

Aidan couldn't help his snort of laughter, though he'd no idea where it came from. It was, of course, entirely inappropriate, and she jerked her arm free of his hold, clearly outraged by his reaction to her pain.

He was making everything worse.

"I'll send Mrs. Liston to you for now," he said hastily, already turning back into the sitting room. "Tomorrow, engage any servants you wish."

And then, mercifully, he was in the passage, with the door closed upon his bride and massive relief in his heart. He would not think of his own sacrifice or hers, only about escape.

THERE WAS SOMETHING blessedly familiar in entering the library to find his brother there, already sitting over a book and a glass of brandy.

"Don't!" Aidan exclaimed, as Patrick, looking horribly guilty, began to speak. "It's done, and we're in the clear. If you ever do anything like that again, I'll beat you to a pulp. There is no more to be said. I don't even want to think about it."

Patrick fell back with a sigh of relief. "Then you don't hate me?"

"I only seem to hate Romilly, and even that isn't fair. Apparently." Aidan sloshed brandy into a glass, walked over to his favourite desk and lifted the pile of waiting letters which he brought with him back to the chair next to his brother's. "Now, what is happening in the world?"

"Prize fight down in Cartside," Patrick said. "Benson and Mullens."

"Oh, that's on, is it? I thought it had been stopped."

"Changed venue to a field in the middle of nowhere. Oh, and there was a duel fought last week, though Scaffy was being too cagey to commit the participants' names to paper. Probably Durward killed his man at last and will have to flee the country."

"After the Mullens fight, presumably," Aidan said, not paying much attention.

"I don't see him missing it. Word is, Snake Sanderly's bolting too."

"Don't see why."

"Society hates him."

"Society is an ass. I never minded Sanderly."

"Only because you've never been on the wrong side of his tongue. You going to take Lady Wolf to Lady Grandison's party?"

"Christ, no." Aidan cast his first letter aside and broke the seal on the second. "When is it?"

"This week, isn't it? I wasn't invited, being a nobody."

"Well, at least you won't be tempted into the deep play that goes on there. Wait a minute—the fight's the day after tomorrow! If I'm not mistaken, Cartside is not so far away from Grand Court. Where's the map?"

"Wish I could go," Patrick said longingly. "To the fight, I mean, not Lady Grandison's."

"Well, you can't," Aidan retorted. "You're rusticating. I'm not." He spread the map out on the desk, confirmed that Grand Court was indeed only a few hours' ride from Cartside, and gave a crow of triumph, "I'll be off first thing."

"First thing?" Patrick stared at him. "But you're just back! Your wife—"

"My wife is mistress of Wolverton Hall. Let her enjoy it. I'm sure as hell going to enjoy my escape. I've earned it!"

# Chapter Four

Eve woke to the sound of clunking crockery, and the sight of a little maid setting a cup and saucer on her bedside table.

"Coffee, my lady. It's what his lordship likes, but I can fetch you a cup of tea if you prefer it."

Heavy with lack of sleep—she had lain awake for hour after restless hour—it took her a moment to fit yesterday's awful events to the present.

She struggled to sit up. "Thank you. Coffee is fine." She took a quick, suspicious glance beyond the maid and was relieved to see no sign of her husband. "Is his lordship up already? Is he at breakfast?"

After all, there had been moments last night of some kind of rapprochement. Not many, admittedly, but enough to give her hope that they might at least become friends in time. And then there had been that odd moment when she'd run into him in the doorway, and he had held her arm in a firm yet gentle grip. His touch had felt curiously...electric. There had been an odd, tingling sensation in her stomach, just because he was so good to look at. Though such silly thoughts would not help her now.

"No, my lady," the maid was saying. "He breakfasted early and rode out first thing."

"Ah. Thank you."

The maid scurried off, leaving Eve to her own thoughts. She and Lord Wolf had at least agreed to make the best of their bargain. She was good at that. She would make Wolverton Hall into a comfortable home for both of them, and she would begin today.

First, she would discuss with him the most urgent repairs and renovations. Perhaps he would even accompany her around the house and thus give her an idea of his tastes and preferences. After that, she could make proper plans and engage more servants for there clearly were not enough to keep a house of this size.

How fortunate that she was practically inclined.

She threw back the covers and prepared for the day, washing in cool water and dressing in her no-nonsense day gown that she normally wore for visits to the sick and the orphans.

And thinking of orphans, she would find the right time to speak to Lord Wolf about his unused house near Covent Garden.

Liston, the ageing butler whom she encountered at the foot of the staircase, directed her to the breakfast parlour.

"Thank you," she said. "Would you ask Mrs. Liston to come to me there in an hour?"

"My lady." He almost creaked when he bowed. The man needed a pension and a cottage.

In the breakfast parlour, Patrick Wolf was tucking into a plate of bacon and eggs and mushrooms. He rose immediately.

"Good morning, my lady. Would you care to choose your own breakfast, or shall I bring you something?"

"No, please sit and enjoy your own. I shall help myself."

There was only one other place set on his right, so she sat down there with her toast and egg and poured herself more coffee from the pot on the table.

"Cream?" Patrick asked with a hint of nervousness.

"No, thank you."

"Did you sleep well?" he asked, his civility almost painful.

"Perfectly," she lied. "Thank you. When will his lordship be back?"

An expression of profound relief relaxed his face. "Oh, you know about that already! He shouldn't be gone more than three weeks."

Eve dropped her hands into her lap and stared at him. "Three weeks? Then he hasn't just gone for a ride?"

The hunted look was back in his eyes. "No, my lady. He's gone to Lady Grandison's party via... well, he's gone. An engagement of long-standing," he added anxiously.

"I'm sure," Eve said sardonically. Anger at such cavalier treatment was beginning to pierce her sense of desolation. Thankfully. "Via where?"

Patrick sighed. "A prize fight. You wouldn't like it."

"No, I wouldn't. I daresay I wouldn't care for Lady Grandison's party either."

"That's what Aidan thought."

She had almost forgotten her husband's Christian name. What did it matter? She was unlikely to have cause—or opportunity—to use it. So much for rapprochement. Just when she'd thought he had run out of ways, or even of desire, to insult her, he had done it again. There had been no need to bolt quite so offensively fast.

He must really hate her.

Part of her cringed at that, but again anger was her saviour. The man was a coward, a louse, unable to take responsibility for his actions or their results. She despised him cordially.

"Then I shall have to proceed without him. Perhaps you will know. Is the house structurally sound? What urgent repairs are necessary?"

"Quite sound, I believe," Patrick said, sounding surprised. "Aidan has always seen to that and made sure the tenants' cottages are watertight."

"Then I can learn the rest of what I need to from Mrs. Liston. There will be some upheaval, I'm afraid, while I bring the house into some order, but I'm afraid I refuse to live in this level of discomfort."

She drained her coffee cup, and, having eaten barely a mouthful of toast and egg, stood up and excused herself. Instead of waiting for Mrs.

Liston, she went down to the kitchen to beard her there. It was a sensible place to begin.

BY THE END OF THAT first week, she had the whole house thoroughly cleaned and aired. She had engaged three more girls from the village to act as housemaids and two footmen for the heavy lifting. She had obtained estimates from painters, decorators and carpenters, and bespoke the services of those she considered best.

The following day, they began their work, leaving Eve with little to do except supervise. And think.

Her aunt had sent on the rest of her possessions from London so she was now equipped with all the clothes and jewels necessary for a lady to make calls and attend parties. But she knew no one but Patrick and the tenants he had taken her to visit at her request. She took note of who was ill, expecting a child, or struggling, realizing with relief that at least part of her duties were very similar to the charitable work she had undertaken in London with Mr. Neville. Of whom she would not think.

Patrick also took her to the vicarage and to the squire's house where she caused quite a stir. Some rumour of his lordship's sudden marriage must have reached them already and the squire, his wife, son and daughters seemed to be unsure whether to be friendly, haughty, or disapproving. They seemed surprised that she spoke the king's English.

The visit depressed her, and anger rose once again that Lord Wolf had left her to face these challenges alone. No doubt he considered it her just deserts for daring to marry him as well as being the source of his twelve thousand pounds.

Wolverton Hall smelled of paint and few of the rooms were comfortable. There was little enough she could do here until their work was done.

In which case, she might as well begin on the new orphanage. Which, unfortunately, required the permission of her husband before she could view it, let alone make the necessary alterations and install the orphans.

A new, rather deliciously vengeful idea began to form. It made her smile, so she went in search of Patrick.

"Where does Lady Grandison reside?"

SHE TRAVELLED BY POST-chaise, since there were no suitable horses to pull the ancient travelling coach she discovered in the carriage house.

Patrick, though he had looked appalled by her decision, at least offered to accompany her. She turned him down, which she could tell was a relief, although he still did his best to dissuade her.

"You ought to give him some notice," he said at last.

"Oh no. Such staid civilities are not his style, are they?"

"I know he ought to have informed you before he left…" Patrick began awkwardly.

"He *ought* to have informed my father he would not be attending his wedding breakfast. He *ought* to have informed me we were leaving London the same day. He *ought* to have informed the newspapers of our nuptials as he promised my father he would. By all I have learned from him, as the dutiful wife of a noble gentleman, I know *exactly* how to behave. I should not be gone above a couple of nights. You won't have time to miss me."

Although she spoke with sardonic humour, Patrick said, "Actually, I will. You deserve better than us."

His words actually softened her anger, if not her intent. She thought resolutely about the orphans and steeled herself once more to obtain what she needed.

IT WAS AN EXHAUSTING journey and almost six in the evening by the time the post-chaise pulled up on the gravel drive before the front door of Grand Court, a gracious, neo-classical pile of daunting proportions. She supposed it was no bigger than Wolverton Hall, but everything about it gleamed, from the walls and windows, to the shining lake glimpsed through the trees and the manicured lawns that surrounded the house.

She stepped down from the chaise with aid of a footman, who had hurried out from the house, and sailed in the open front door as if she had every right to be there. Which was when she realized she had mistimed everything.

For some reason, she had thought they would all be at dinner at six. It was when her family ate, though she was aware that fashionable people dined later. At Wolverton Hall, after the first night, they also dined at six, which Patrick called "country hours" because, he said, there was nothing else to do in the country but eat and sleep.

Grand Court was clearly more fashionable. People were milling about the front hall and the elegant curved staircase, still in morning dress. Eve realized with dismay that they were probably retiring to change before dining.

A much scarier butler than either her father's or Liston, gazed at her with raised brows, his hand held out for her card—which, of course, she did not have.

"I'm Lady Wolf," she said into the sudden silence of the hallway.

A smart, middle-aged lady who was bustling forward to meet her—no doubt Lady Grandison herself—paused involuntarily before continuing in clear astonishment. A nightmare of whispers echoed around her, and she tilted her chin to give herself courage.

And then she saw the man on the stairs, staring at her in undisguised horror.

Her husband.

*"I'M LADY WOLF."*

The voice as much as the words vibrated through Aidan with shock. He spun around on the stairs and there she stood, just inside the front door, facing the butler and Lady Grandison.

The heat of embarrassment burned into his face—before he realized this was no naïve stumbling on her part. There was defiance in her eyes as they briefly met his. And, surely triumph.

She knew exactly what she was doing.

Lady Grandison, ever the perfect hostess, held out her hand, exclaiming, "What a delightful surprise!"

Aidan clenched his teeth. His first instinct was to roar at her to get out of here where she was neither invited nor wanted. His second was to give her the cut direct and walk away, leaving her to the tender mercies of the Grandisons and their guests. Including, he thought savagely, Snake Sanderly.

But he could do neither of these things without showing himself in an appalling light. She had done enough of that already in turning up where he had not bothered to tell anyone he was married. He hadn't wanted to think about it, let alone talk about it.

And that look in his wife's eyes showed him she understood perfectly.

So he played the only hand he could and descended the stairs with a smile of welcome on his lips.

Lady Grandison slapped his hand with her fan. "How dare you keep this charming secret from us, Wolf?"

Aidan took his wife's gloved hand, still smiling. "You see, my dear, how you have spoiled my surprise? I forgive you, since I am overjoyed to see you. Allow me to make you known to your hostess, Lady Grandison. Now, come with me. I want you to myself for a little before you will meet everyone at dinner."

Her breath caught, for she knew damned well why he wanted her alone and it was not going to be pleasant. He placed her hand firmly in his arm and tugged her inexorably toward the stairs.

However, she dug in her heels a moment longer to turn courteously back to Lady Grandison. "I hope your ladyship will forgive my unannounced arrival—"

"Oh, you are forgiven, Lady Wolf. It's your husband I have the problem with! Not a word about his marriage!"

"I shall not stay above an hour," Eve said. "I merely wished—"

"That, I will *not* forgive! I assure you we are quite used to people coming and going unexpectedly. You are a most welcome addition to our party, Lady Wolf. We all look forward to making your acquaintance."

Aidan swept her upstairs like the over-eager bridegroom he most certainly was not, and through the long passages to his room, where he threw open the door. He almost hurled her inside, before closing the door and leaning against it, glaring at her.

"Revenge, my lady?" he said harshly. "Is it not enough that you have my name, my title and home, that you must em—"

"Frankly, no," she interrupted calmly. "It is not enough. If you will stop whining about your sad difficulties—which you brought entirely upon yourself—I will explain to you how you may actually do some good in the world."

His spurt of temper cut off like a tap. *Whining?* Why that word should rankle more than any other, he did not know, but it certainly conjured an image of himself he did not like. Besides, he was aware he should not have abandoned her without a word in a strange house the day after he married her. He doubted she had anything to do with her father's trickery, and although she benefitted from social promotion in becoming Baroness Wolf, she had stepped out of her own society and her own life, and been forced to give up the man she had wished to marry.

It was odd of her, of course, to choose an ageing vicar when surely much more personable and wealthy young men would have been desperate to ally with her family if not to Eve herself. But then, she was an odd creature, as he was only just discovering.

"Sit down," he muttered, brushing past her, "and be comfortable."

She took off her hat and pelisse, but sat down with them on her lap, as though she had no intention of staying.

*Good.*

He poured himself a small brandy from the decanter on the dresser, and at the last minute cocked one eyebrow at her. She shook her head.

"I did not come to annoy you," she said boldly, "although I'll admit it was a welcome bonus, but to discuss an urgent matter that I would have brought up at the Hall if you had not fled quite so incontinently."

A breath of amusement took him by surprise. She had a certain style. He allowed her that.

"Let us take the rest of the insults, deserved and otherwise, as read also," he said wryly, echoing their discussion on their wedding day. "What is this urgent matter?"

"I have long been involved with the charitable running of an orphanage. The children are housed in a quite unsuitable building in St. Giles which is full of damp and mould and is too small for the number of orphans. Disease is therefore also a problem."

He frowned. "You do not need my permission to spend your money or your time on charities, or anything else you wish. I am not that kind of a husband."

"In this case, I do need your permission. Mr. Neville has identified a suitable house only a few hundred yards from the old building. Just on the edge of Covent Garden, it stands in a small park, which would also provide some desirable fresh air for the children."

"What is this to do with me?" he asked impatiently.

"The house is to do with you. It belongs to you."

His eyebrows flew up. "It does? Oh! Wait, you mean the place in Grass Square? The area is no longer suitable for a gentleman's town house, but I can't sell it. It's entailed."

"But you can rent it out."

"I can," he said slowly. "Are you telling me, you forced your way in here just to ask me that?"

"No," she snapped. "I called on Lady Grandison to ask you that. Time is of the essence if the children are to be re-housed before the winter. Another winter in the old house will surely kill many."

She was serious. Deeply serious.

"I can't afford the upkeep," he muttered. "Or the repairs."

"We shall take care of that. A nominal rent would be appreciated in return."

He frowned at her, scanning her face, which was not plain at all but alive with enthusiasm and determination. "This truly means much to you."

"It does."

He could see no disadvantage, although her family had fooled him before. "Is your father involved with this orphanage in any way?" he asked suspiciously.

She shook her head. "No. Although he occasionally employs the children, like Georgie the boot boy."

Aidan shrugged. "Do it then. I'll write to my man of business."

"If you would give me the letter now, I can go up to London tomorrow to set things in motion before I return to Wolverton Hall."

"I'll write it this evening or first thing tomorrow," he said impatiently. "But as for your—"

"Now would be better," she interrupted. "Before I depart for the village inn."

He blinked. She gazed back from eyes that were clear and honest and not a little beautiful. She truly intended to put up at the inn.

Which, belatedly, made him aware of all the reasons why she should not.

"Oh, no, my girl," he said dangerously. "You saw fit to come here as my wife, and here you will most definitely stay."

# Chapter Five

"Stay?" Eve repeated, uncomprehending. Having achieved her goal—including the vengeance that had turned out not to be as satisfying as she had imagined—she wished only to be away from here. "Why on earth would I stay? Neither of us wants me here."

His manner had changed again. From the barely suppressed anger with which he had greeted her, he had got distracted and agreed with more bewilderment than fuss to her request. And now the steely stranger was back.

"And yet here you are," he said icily. "So once again, we must make the best of it."

"The best," she said, "is for me to step back into the chaise—with your letter—spend tonight at the inn, and travel to London tomorrow. You will be discommoded no further."

"I cannot make up my mind," Lord Wolf said, looking her up and down, "whether you are naïve or malicious. I have no intention of dealing with the explosion of scandal and gossip that would arise from your departure a mere hour after your unlooked for arrival. It is awkward enough that you chose to appear before my marriage was made public. Now that you *are* here, you will play the devoted wife until we leave together."

"I am not an actress," she said acidly. "And your wishes would challenge even a Mrs. Siddons."

"We are speaking of the ton, my dear wife, not cuddling peasants in some lovers' lane. Your being present is devotion enough. Sharing my room displays the discreet lust of the newlywed. Beyond that, you need not speak to me nor pay me any attention whatsoever."

There was so much offence in that speech that she didn't know where to begin. What came blurting out was, "I shall not share your room!"

He smiled unpleasantly. "And yet here you are. Are you really going to put Lady Grandison to the trouble of conjuring you up another in her already full house? Who would you like to turn out to accommodate you?"

"No one! I shall stay at the inn."

"I cannot allow you to so insult Lady Grandison."

"You mean you cannot allow the insult to *you*," she retorted. "You are merely afraid my departure will be even more embarrassing than my arrival."

"Did I not just say that?"

She curled her lip. "You are afraid of their contempt. You are afraid to appear in an even poorer light than you already have! So afraid that you are even prepared to put your vulgar wife, the mere cit's daughter, on display."

She thought his face paled, though his smile was savage enough.

"It is something of a Hobson's choice. Calm your revulsion with the thought of your father's approval. I am doing my best—again—to promote you in society."

"You are doing your best to punish me," she said hoarsely, "for your own and your brother's faults. I despise you."

"Then we are in perfect accord." A knock sounded on the door and he strode across the room to open it. "And on cue, here is your baggage. Dear me, is this all?"

And suddenly, with her bag on his bed and the departure of the maid, her temper died, and the hot blood drained from her face.

"You see?" she said. "I would only embarrass you further if I stayed. I did not pack for such a purpose. For your comfort, if not for that of the orphans, just give me the letter you promised and let me go."

"Touching," he said with another curl of his lip. "Unpack your bag. Unless you desire me to do so."

She hesitated, and not just because everything in her revolted at obeying such a peremptory order. But he was bound to despise her clothes anyway.

*Despise*. She wished she had not used that word to him. She wished she had not come, for all she had achieved was making a terrible situation worse.

With clumsy hands, she opened the bag and took out her neatly folded gowns which she laid on the bed in a pile.

"Well," he said, without touching them. "That looks like an evening gown. You had best change."

Her gaze flew to his face. God knew what he read in her eyes for he swung away from her saying harshly, "It's why you married me, to go into society. Don't make a fuss. You have ten minutes while I speak to a friend."

And he walked out without a backward glance.

IT WAS THE FEAR IN her eyes that drove him from his room.

Dear God, what was he becoming?

*"I despise you,"* she had said. And no wonder. He despised himself. Whatever he had promised her, he was *not* making the best of their difficult situation. He was allowing his temper to make it worse. He was *bullying* that girl who was entirely alone in a houseful of strangers to whom she considered herself inferior.

Just because he had wanted a couple more weeks of being unencumbered.

Almost at random, he thumped his knuckles against a door in the passage and walked in.

"Good God," Lord Sanderly drawled, "It's the secret bridegroom. Seeking refuge already?"

Snake Sanderly had a tongue like a blade. He was tucking a fine lawn shirt into his close-fitting black pantaloons, his expression one of mere amusement. He was not known as a sympathetic man. Aidan had no idea why he was here except he'd known Snake a long time and never paid much attention to the unlikely calumnies pronounced against him by society.

"I'm a selfish bastard," Aidan said, throwing himself into the nearest chair.

"What do you want? Absolution? I'm not the priestly sort."

"I think I want a kick in the breeches."

"Happy to oblige there." Snake picked up a well starched cravat, wound it around his neck and with a flick of his long fingers seemed to conjure a veritable cascade of folds before accurately placing a plain gold pin to hold the beauty in place.

"You'll be kind to her?" Aidan said abruptly. "Ask Miss Cole to look after her?"

Sanderly, to everyone's surprise—including his own, Aidan suspected—appeared to be engaged to Miss Harriet Cole, the kind-hearted and rather lovely goddaughter of their hostess.

"To save you the trouble?" Snake asked.

"My kindness will hardly be welcome," Aidan said ruefully. "In any case, I'm bound to be seated nowhere near her. Lady Grandison will oblige you if you ask."

"Some terribly kind person is still bound to tell her about Mrs. Archer."

And that was a complication Aidan had not even thought of. Mrs. Archer, his occasional mistress, had been no more than a pleasant flirtation so far at Grand Court, but he had been regarding her more intimate favours as a treat to look forward to before the end of the party. He rather suspected Mrs. Archer was doing the same.

Aidan swore. "I can't even ask you to take her off my hands."

"Even were I remotely inclined, I would not oblige you there. I suppose you married the girl for her money. Patrick being horribly dipped."

Aidan's face heated. "I don't want that said either, though I suppose the world will know it."

"One can't control gossip," Sanderly said, reaching for his coat. "All you can do is rise above it."

No one knew that better than Snake.

"She came to me about a matter she considered urgent," Aidan said. "And now she wants to stay at the inn. She has no escort."

Snake's thin lips twitched. "Astonishing how proper you married men suddenly become. Do you want rid of her?"

*Yes.* But more than that... "I want her to be safe," he muttered. "Including from malicious tongues."

"Then you rather went the wrong way about it. You've been here a week and never said a word about her. Society will just *love* the story of how she just appeared at Lady Grandison's party. Trust me it will be most of the way round the country by tomorrow."

"Then I'm right to keep her here," Aidan said, frowning. "And after tomorrow's ball, we can leave together in perfect harmony." At least publicly. He stood up. "Thanks, Snake."

Snake said nothing, but Aidan suspected as he went out, that the man was vastly amused.

Allowing his wife rather more courtesy than he had given Sanderly, Aidan knocked at his own door and waited until her voice bade him enter before he went in.

She stood before the looking glass in her modest evening gown, jabbing pins into her hair which she had scraped back with ruthless severity.

"Oh the devil," he said, irritably, striding up behind her. Alarm entered her eyes in the glass, and then outrage as he swept both hands through her hair sending pins flying in all directions. "Why do you do that to yourself?"

"Convenience," she retorted. "I would rather be neat than ridiculous."

Aidan did not answer, for he was suddenly distracted by the thick softness of her hair. He barely remembered how it had looked at their few previous meetings because he had hardly glanced at her. Concerned with his own dignity in an intolerable situation, he had not considered her at all.

"I regret my ill-manners and my hasty words," he said in a rush. "I have an abominable temper, for which I apologize."

Surprise widened her profound dark eyes.

Without conscious thought, he picked up her hairbrush and stroked it through her silken hair. "It really will be better for everyone concerned if you stay here tonight and tomorrow night. Your existence and your appearance will thus cause considerably less gossip than if you bolt again as if I have thrown you out."

He caught her sardonic expression. "Yes, it would look bad of me," he admitted. "But it is you who will ultimately be blamed. The woman always is. It isn't fair but it is reality. For both our sakes, endure this evening and tomorrow and we can leave together the day after the ball."

"*Ball?*" she said, fresh alarm spiking in her eyes. "I have nothing suitable to wear for a ball!"

"We will manage," he said firmly. In truth, his attention was not on such details but in coaxing her hair into the shape that suited her features and her nature.

"But I wanted to begin the renovation of the house to receive the orphans..."

"Unless you plan to do your own labouring, you can surely leave that in the hands of others. Write to whoever you need to, to put him in touch with my man of business and we can send both epistles in the morning."

She held herself rigid under his ministrations, but now whether through agreement with his plan for the orphans or admiration of her changing reflection in the glass, she began to relax.

"Jewels," he said brusquely, when he had placed the last pin. He was oddly reluctant to stop touching her.

She spun away from him, muttering, "I only have pearls with me."

"They'll do."

Having extracted them from the bag, she fastened them herself without even glancing again in the mirror.

"You should wear emeralds," he said.

She cast him a quick, startled glance.

"Another time," he said hastily. "You had best wait for me, so if you don't wish your wifely modesty to be offended, avert your gaze."

She fled to the window, where she stared resolutely outward while he discarded his day clothes, washed, and re-dressed.

His cravat lacked Sanderly's elegance. But it would do.

They would both do.

ENTIRELY DISCONCERTED by her husband's clever fingers in her hair, Eve could do little more than hold her neutral expression while her blood warmed and her scalp tingled to his touch. It entered her head that he was far too practiced at dressing and pinning a lady's hair—an odd skill for a nobleman. When he brushed against her neck, her breath caught at the shock of it.

Gazing out of the window, while he splashed and rustled behind her, tension rose. She had to fight the urge to turn and watch him. This was all far too...intimate. It gave her butterflies in her stomach.

And yet she did not dislike it. She did not dislike *him* when he was being reasonable.

He had apologized. Should she not do the same?

He stood beside her, smelling clean and fresh, his arm winged. "Lady Wolf."

"Lord Wolf," she managed in the same, light tone, and laid her hand on his arm. She drew in a breath as they walked together. "I apologize for my own temper." *I don't despise you at all.* But before she could say the words, he spoke again.

"There is no need. My behaviour would enrage a saint. Let us talk no more of the matter and be more courteous in the future. Will you cope with a formal dinner?"

Was that his way of asking if she knew which cutlery to use, and when to leave the dining room? Her difficulties were not with manners but with people. But she would never admit that.

"I believe so," she said calmly.

She had endured many of her father's large, formal dinners and those of his friends. She assured herself this one was no harder and walked silently by his side down the staircase and into a large, crowded salon where a footman offered them sherry in fine glasses.

She was glad to take one. It gave her something to concentrate on while everyone turned and gawped at her. Unfortunately, she was cursed with sharp hearing and many among the Quality had no concept of lowering their voices.

"She's Wolf's new baroness. Now why did he keep her so secret?"

"Do you suppose Helena Archer knows?"

"At least she *looks* like a lady. Does she smell of the shop?"

"No, but she probably *sounds* of it. No wonder she doesn't open her mouth."

Not the kind of comments guaranteed to boost one's confidence. Fortunately, she had no interest in them, and Wolf drew her straight past them and further into the dazzling room. She had been among wealthy before. She had grown up with them, had friends among them. But these people seemed to radiate innate superiority, as if they didn't even need to think about it. Or perhaps that was just her sudden timidity.

If she was to do her duty by her husband, and by her family, these were the people she would need to be familiar with. And yet there seemed nothing open about them at all.

Under everyone's gaze, Lord Wolf halted beside two lovely young ladies, the most elegant man she had ever seen, and a stocky man with an amiable smile.

"Thought you'd like to meet my wife," Wolf said casually. "Eve, Lady Barbara Martindale, Miss Cole who is Lady Grandison's goddaughter, Lord Sanderly—Lady Bab's brother—and Mr. Martindale."

Mr. Martindale was the amiable man, presumably Lady Barbara's husband. Lord Sanderly the elegant one with the haughty, rather terrifying expression and the most amazing blue eyes she had ever seen.

Lady Bab, at least, did not appear to be scary at all. If her open gaze was curious, her smile was friendly and she offered her hand at once.

"Lady Wolf, a pleasure to make your acquaintance. What a brave lady you are to take on our untamed Wolf! I have to tell you, I was madly in love with him for the entire first month of my come-out."

"Were you?" Wolf said in surprise. "Then you hid it very well!"

"I was probably too overwhelmed to speak to you."

"Are you sure you're not thinking of someone else?" Wolf said.

Lady Bab laughed. "Of course not! You do cut quite the dash, you know. Only then I met James and forgot all about you."

Mr. Martindale looked more stoic than gratified by this accolade—and indeed Eve found it hard to believe that he could have eclipsed Lord Wolf in an impressionable maidenly breast. But then, physical appearance was not everything.

It was very odd, though, that even among these friendly strangers, surrounded by a multitude of others, she felt the urge to cling to her husband whom she scarcely knew any better. But in this company, he was all that was familiar.

Miss Cole invited her for a morning walk to see the countryside. "Though I warn you, my sisters and cousin might join us and that is not always peaceful."

"I shall be happy to make their acquaintance."

"Not at that time of the morning," Lord Sanderly murmured. "One needs fortitude."

"They're children," Wolf said, as though that explained everything.

"Of an extremely lively nature," Miss Cole added. "Even Lily when she is well."

During these exchanges, Eve happened to glance at Mr. Martindale and glimpsed over his shoulder, a beautiful, fair lady. She had been sweeping alone through the room but now paused beside another woman. Both gazed right at her.

The fair lady curled her lip, took her companion's arm, and walked on. A taste, no doubt, of what Eve would have to endure for the rest of the evening, to say nothing of tomorrow night's ball which was now the subject of discussion among her immediate companions.

"It's to be quite a grand affair," Miss Cole said to her, with a hint of surprising anxiety. "I believe most of the county has been invited."

By which she no doubt meant all the gently born families. A strong pang of longing engulfed Eve, for Mr. Neville and an unassuming, busy life among the poor, the troubled, and the lonely, doing good and making a difference...

Her sad musings were interrupted by Lady Grandison, who bustled up to her. "Oh good, you've met Sanderly. I've given him this evening's honour of taking you in to dine. Feel free to be as rude as you like to him!"

She passed on with a distracted smile, leaving Eve with her face burning. Did everyone expect her to have no manners? Just because of her parents' lowly birth?

No one else seemed to find anything unusual in Lady Grandison's advice, and in any case, there was a general movement of couples behind her ladyship and an elderly gentleman, presumably toward the dining room.

Lord Sanderly was offering her his arm. She knew an urge to flee, or to cling to Lord Wolf's arm instead. One impulse was as ridiculous as the other.

She placed the tips of her fingers on Sanderly's arm and walked rather blindly at his side.

"The barb was aimed at me, not you," he murmured unexpectedly. "The world knows me as offensive, and rudeness in return is really the only answer."

"She does not like you?" Eve asked, shocked.

"I see no reason why she should, but she is coming around since I intend to marry her goddaughter."

Intrigued by this admittedly alarming man, Eve forgot to be afraid. And indeed, he proved to be an amusing companion, conversing humorously on light, impersonal subjects that put her at her ease.

"You and Lord Wolf are friends of long standing?" she asked over the soup course.

"We've known each other since school, though our lives went in different directions thereafter."

"How so?"

He gave a little shrug. "Wolf inherited his title early. I made a career in the army. For a time."

Although she baulked at first at the idea of him as a soldier, when she looked again at his hard, intelligent eyes and uncompromising chin, it began to make sense.

"When I came home, I tended my own acres, as Wolf tends to his."

She must have betrayed her surprise for lazy amusement glinted in his eyes.

"You don't imagine Wolf as a farmer?"

"I imagined him more as a...a man about town," she said lightly, then wondered if she should really be admitting to knowing her husband so little.

"I believe he drops into Town for the Season and a couple of country parties a year. I met him at the races once. And the recent prize fight, of course, though I probably should not tell you that."

Then everyone knew she had been deserted for a prize fight? It was a better reason than him being unable to stand the sight of his wife.

The servants removed the soup plates and some delicious-smelling fish, glistening in herb butter was placed in front of her.

The gentleman on her other side turned to her and introduced himself as Mr. Archer.

Was that not a name she had overheard among the gossips when she had first entered the salon?

"You, I know, are Lady Wolf," he said. "Everyone is agog to meet you."

"I'm sure his lordship planned it that way," she said lightly.

Mr. Archer, a youngish, rather petulant-looking man with flaring nostrils, raised his eyebrows. "Do you really think so? How quaint you are."

Her hackles rising, she looked him in the eye. "You do not approve of me, sir?"

"My dear lady! On the contrary, both your existence and your presence at Grand Court delight me."

"I fail to see why," she said, forcing a smile to her lips at this odd fervour. After all, though she would far rather be rude to this gentleman than to Lord Sanderly whom she rather liked, she had been brought up to be courteous.

"Bless your innocent heart." Mr. Archer leaned closer and she smelled brandy as well as wine on his breath. He lowered his voice confidingly. "Because it removes the scandal from my house to yours, of course."

*What scandal*? Fortunately she did not ask aloud, and in any case, Archer's attention was claimed by the lady on his other side.

She turned to Sanderly and found his watchful gaze fixed just beyond her, on Archer.

"Who is he?" she murmured. "Another friend of Lord Wolf's?"

"No," Sanderly said. His eyes dropped to hers. "He is something of a gossip. You would be wise to pay him little attention."

# Chapter Six

At first Aidan found it rather a humorous and deserved irony that although Sanderly sat at one side of his wife, Helena's husband had been placed at the other.

Only then he considered what Archer's spite might make him say and, more to the point, how this might humiliate Eve.

He did not flatter himself that she cared whose bed he slept in—so long as it wasn't hers—but it couldn't be pleasant for her to learn this piece of gossip, no doubt spiced up by Archer's malice. Aidan should have warned her, though his mind rather boggled at explaining the situation to his clearly innocent young wife.

"I'll tell you what," he muttered to Sanderly, taking the seat next to him once the ladies had withdrawn and the port had been passed around the table, "this marriage business is more complicated than it looks."

"Are you warning me off the institution?" Sanderly inquired.

"Lord, no. Your case is different." He gave a quick, rueful smile. "Truth to tell, yours is the kind of case I rather imagined for myself in a few years. A young lady who was suitable, pretty, and congenial, to court and marry." Under Sanderly's sardonic gaze, he suddenly remembered Alicia Eldridge and gave a twisted smile of apology. "Sorry. I suppose our situations are not so different after all. What did you say to get rid of her?"

Sanderly did not ask who or what he meant. "Nothing."

"Nothing? Forgive the intrusion, but does your Miss Cole know of your past—er...entanglements?"

In anyone else, he might have imagined a faint flush rising to the cheeks. “Miss Cole knows my past is no threat.”

Wolf sighed. “*That* is the difference. I’m not much used to discretion.”

“You don’t say so,” Sanderly drawled.

“Damn it, I’ve told you how things are. Mine is a marriage of convenience. I just don’t want to humiliate the girl.”

“How very touching.”

Actually, it was. Aidan, unused to considering other people at all—let alone those who had been tied to him by trickery like a millstone around his neck—found, against his will that he felt responsible for Eve. With regret, he saw his anticipated bout of lusty pleasures vanishing from his grasp.

Because of the ball the following evening, which would go on into the early hours, it was assumed everyone would want an early night and plenty of rest. So Aidan knew he would have to be quick in finding a moment to speak to Helena.

For once, fortune favoured him. As the gentlemen made their way to the drawing room to rejoin the ladies, he caught sight of Helena’s graceful figure rounding the curve of the staircase from the landing above.

He hung back, letting the others precede him, and then walked back to Helena.

“Well, well,” she drawled. “Escaping the little wife already?”

“Not at this precise moment,” Aidan said, well aware that his entire bolt to Grand Court, via the exciting prize fight where he’d won a hundred guineas by wagering on the better man, had been about escaping his wife. “In fact, I want to talk to you about her.”

“Shockingly bad ton, Aidan. Or must I call you *my lord* again?”

“You can call me anything you like so long as you don’t upset my wife.”

A flush rose up her neck, mottling her usually perfect skin. "I assure you I have no intention of *speaking* to your wife. She has no ton at all." And she swept rapidly into the drawing room.

Aidan followed more slowly. The conversation had not gone quite as he had planned. In fact, he perceived he had offended Helena—her pride, not her heart which he knew instinctively had been no more involved than his in their pleasurable relationship. He preferred to be on good terms with everyone, so he thought seriously about sitting beside her and trying to make things right. However, he had got what he needed from her, a promise not to embarrass his wife, so it seemed safest not to rock that particular boat. Not until he had had a chance to explain to his wife.

LIKE EVERYONE ELSE in the drawing room, Miss Harriet Cole, seated beside the new Lady Wolf, saw Helena Archer re-enter the drawing room only a few seconds behind the gentlemen. She looked rather flushed and agitated. And only a few steps behind her, came Lord Wolf.

She felt a spurt of irritation. Normally, she rather liked Wolf. He was charming and good-natured, and had never, to her knowledge, spoken against her beloved Sanderly. She had been glad to accept her betrothed's request that she look after the new Lady Wolf, having a certain empathy for outsiders in a society which was still new to her. And she knew the source of the request was Wolf himself.

However, she found she rather liked her ladyship on her own account. She was shy and quiet, certainly, but she had a quick sense of humour that made her eyes laugh. But seriously, how dare Wolf ask for their help with his struggling new wife, while he himself cavorted so indiscreetly with his mistress?

Hopefully, the girl had not noticed. But when Harriet turned to her, a bright remark on her lips about the music they had been discussing, she saw that Lady Wolf was looking straight at Mrs. Archer.

Her ladyship dropped her gaze immediately, her long chestnut lashes veiling her eyes. But not before Harriet had glimpsed a very odd expression indeed. It seemed to contain dawning understanding, and something else that looked almost…stricken.

Ignoring Harriet's remark, she asked, "Is that lady who just entered Mrs. Archer?"

"Yes," Harriet said uneasily. "Why?"

"No reason. Except I sat beside her husband at dinner. Have you attended the opera at Covent Garden then?"

Harriet allowed the subject change, but she now had an additional reason to look forward to her moonlight stroll with Sanderly. This had become a habit since their betrothal a matter of days ago. No doubt everyone knew, but even Lady Grandison turned a blind eye to the impropriety, since they would be married very soon.

With a little shiver of anticipation, Harriet rose as the company began to break up and made her way to the back terrace where her betrothed awaited her. Although her heart melted when his face lit up, she grasped his arm with unusual briskness and began to march rather than stroll toward the maze.

"What is Wolf up to?" she fumed. "He is the one who should be looking after her and yet he flaunts his mistress in her face."

"Hardly," Sanderly said mildly. "I rather think he was trying to ensure her co-operation in his discretion."

"Well he managed to achieve the opposite!"

"Ah. She noticed then?"

"Oh, she noticed."

He closed his warm fingers over hers on his arm. "Don't break your heart over it, Harriet. Theirs is a marriage of convenience. I daresay they will rub along together well enough in time, but for now their hearts are hardly engaged. And believe me, Wolf had no time to tumble anyone."

"Oh," said Harriet, who was still rather vague on what tumbling entailed, though she looked forward to learning. "Perhaps she was just angry then."

"It seems likely. And *her* heart is not engaged either."

Harriet considered this for a moment. "What makes you think Lady Wolf is indifferent to her husband?"

He shrugged. "She doesn't know him well enough to be anything else. She even refers to him as *Lord Wolf*, not as *Wolf* or *Aidan* or even *my husband*, as though they were complete strangers. I would doubt they have had any but the shallowest of conversations, and not many of those."

"Poor girl," Harriet murmured, trying to imagine the awfulness, the fear, of being married to a complete stranger. Or any man, really, who was not Sanderly. A husband had such power over his wife...

"Are you easy on the matter now?" Sanderly asked.

They entered the maze gate, and turned toward the bench on the left, immediately behind the high hedge. Sanderly took her into his arms and butterflies soared in her stomach and her veins. But she caught his face between her hands to halt whatever he intended.

"No. I'm not easy, Serp. There is more to this. Some part of Lady Wolf's heart *is* engaged. I saw it in her eyes."

He regarded her in silence for a few moments. "There's no point in telling you not to interfere in their business, is there?"

"Not *interfere*," she said unclearly. "But...don't you want to help Lord Wolf?"

"No," Sanderly said frankly. "I'd much rather kiss you."

And since that suited Harriet entirely, she returned his embrace and lost herself in her own love.

WHILE CHATTER AND LAUGHTER went on all around her, Eve tried to maintain a faint smile and an attentive expression. But she hardly heard a word.

She felt utterly confused and not a little shocked. In her world, respectability—not merely the appearance of it—was all, and adultery was plainly wrong. In response to some criticism of their aunt's, Miranda had once scoffed that the aristocracy cared nothing for such petty bourgeois morality. And it seemed she was right.

If Lord Wolf loved Mrs. Archer, it explained some of his ferocity at being "forced" into marriage. And why he had bolted to this party, told no one of his marriage, and been so angry that Eve had followed him. He had come to tell Mrs. Archer first.

It seemed Eve was not the only one who had lost someone in this marriage she should never have allowed.

Not that Mrs. Archer appeared to be lost to him. They had clearly enjoyed some kind of encounter before walking separately into the drawing room. If Eve had needed confirmation, Harriet Cole's anxious observation provided it.

It was not surprising. Little more than a week ago, Lord Wolf had been a young bachelor with a certain careless, restless charm that was no doubt appealing to many women. His temper seemed somewhat erratic, but that, Eve suspected, was her fault, for everyone else she had met regarded him as amiable and good-humoured.

So she pitied him a little for his tragic love for Mrs. Archer, even while she disapproved. And she *hurt* somewhere, though she couldn't quite understand how or why. Marriages of convenience left a trail of sadness in their wake. And considering Mrs. Archer's unpleasant husband, no wonder she had fallen for Lord Wolf. Perhaps their love was of long-standing.

Either way, the question remained, what should Eve do about it? Pretend she didn't know? Avert her eyes and say nothing? Sooner or later she and Mrs. Archer would be thrown together, and for some reason that appalled her. Mrs. Archer must hate her. The rest of the party clearly knew about the affair and were either laughing at Eve—the plain wife married for her money—or pitied her. They already despised her for her birth.

In the midst of all these people, she had never felt more alone.

She folded one arm across her stomach as though to quell the source of pain.

*Pride. It is only pride.*

That being so, what should she do?

*Nothing.*

Only doing nothing was alien to her nature. She wished she knew what kind of woman Mrs. Archer was. If she was worthy of Wolf. Once she knew that, perhaps she would see her way clear. Besides, her pride rather demanded that she show the world, especially her husband, that she cared nothing for the existence of a mistress.

Snapping herself out of her reverie, she realized that people were beginning to say goodnight and retire. Searching for Lord Wolf, she saw him at the other side of the room, making his way toward her.

It was now or never. She rose, moving swiftly away from him toward the window, where Mrs. Archer still sat among her friends. What excuse did she have for approaching a stranger?

*Good evening, Mrs. Archer. I believe you are a friend of my husband's.*

Hardly, everyone here appeared to be his friend. She should turn away now...

But Mrs. Archer rose from her window seat, laughing at something that had been said. Beginning to walk away she glanced back over her shoulder to add some rejoinder, and Eve had her excuse to stop for fear of them walking into each other.

And suddenly all eyes were upon them. Mrs. Archer's companions became suddenly aware of her and developed avid expressions of anticipation. The noise in the room seemed to quieten, but no doubt that was Eve's over-sensitive imagination.

Mrs. Archer halted too, and, slowly followed the direction of her friends' attention.

Eve smiled. "Excuse my clumsiness—I almost walked into you. I'm Lady Wolf."

She saw her mistake at once. There was no softening, no timidity or shame in the hard eyes that met hers. Instead, there was a flare of something very like triumph.

Mrs. Archer looked her up and down without hurry. She twitched one lip with clear contempt and was clearly about to turn away.

*The cut direct*. The most fearsome social weapon known to man. Or woman. Eve's blood ran suddenly cold.

And then an arm slid through hers.

"There you are," Lord Wolf said beside her. "You must be exhausted after your journey, so let us retire. Good night, all."

"Good night," Eve managed and was whisked away with faint echoes following her.

Lord Wolf's grip was like steel, his body rigid as he swept her through those lingering in the drawing room and those making their way across the landing to the staircase. Despite the faint smile on his lips, and the odd word thrown to friends and acquaintances, his eyes were as harsh and dark as a stormy sky.

Inexorably, he all but marched her upstairs and along the passage to his bedchamber. He must have looked like an eager bridegroom, only Eve knew the truth.

He was furious because she had erred in some way she didn't quite understand.

As soon as they entered the room, he kicked the door shut and all but threw her from him. A lamp had been lit but turned down low. It only emphasized the darkness of his face.

Fury blazed out of his eyes. In those moments, she knew he hated her.

"What in God's name were you thinking?" he hissed between clenched teeth. "Are you determined to shame us both?"

The injustice of that took her breath away, causing disastrous words to burst from her lips.

"It is not I conducting a public affair with a married woman under the nose of my despised spouse. And hers."

"More revenge? You imbecile! You opened yourself to be truly despised. You were *this* close to the cut direct!" He threw up his finger and thumb, almost touching. "And everyone saw it! We will be laughing stocks."

"You mean *you* might be," she retorted. "I already am one."

"And no wonder! Have you *no* idea how to go on?"

"Clearly not. You should have listened to me at the outset and allowed me to stay at the inn—which rather makes *you* the imbecile." She swung away from him, appalled by her own childish words which were greeted with stony, seething silence.

"Go to bed," he flung at her at last, like a parent to a naughty child.

Two swift footsteps, behind her, the sound of the door wrenching open and closing with little attempt not to slam it. And then his steps fading, the sound of his distant voice exchanging friendly words with others.

But not with her, never with her.

Tears ran down her cheeks. She wiped them absently with the backs of her hands, then changed out of her evening gown with some difficulty. In her nightgown and robe, after a cursory wash, she found a spare blanket in the cupboard and curled up with it on the sofa at the foot of his bed.

Despair swamped her.

THE COSY SALON NEXT to the library had been given over to those gentlemen who retired and rose late, even in the country. A fire was lit to stave off the night chill, and card tables were permanently set up for the guests' entertainment.

Play at the Grandisons' parties was traditionally deep and Aidan had so far avoided it. But the room and the company were convivial, and in his rage he had nowhere else to go unless he strode out into the darkness, which, God knew, was tempting.

However, even by the time he reached the salon, his temper was cooling and he was aware, yet again, that he had been unfair to her. He had rescued her from Helena's cut direct in the nick of time, and in truth, his anger had been largely against Helena—and himself for not paying close enough attention. He should not even have been surprised, let alone annoyed, by Eve's ignorance of society's unspoken conventions. She had no one but him to teach her and he, careless to a fault, took the oddities of his class far too much for granted. He had grown up with them, with friends and uncles to keep him right as a very young man.

Eve, without a mother or experience, was understandably ignorant. The knowledge that he had no right to blame her did not help his temper. He could not be in the same room as her right now.

Gritting his teeth on the thought that there was only one more day of this torment to go, he opened the door of the salon and stepped in to the cosy glow.

Some tobacco smoke from a pipe or two and even a cigarillo, hung in the air.

"Wolf!" The cry went up from a few of the occupants. Someone even let forth a wolf-howl, an old joke from his one year at Oxford. Others raised their glasses to him in more decorous welcome.

Aidan smiled by way of acknowledgment and went to pour himself a glass of brandy. He needed it.

Unusually, Snake was present, perhaps combatting the lusts of the flesh. Harriet Cole was good for him. He was not quite so free with his devastating tongue, which lacked the edge of viciousness that had made him both feared and fascinating. In fact, he was in danger of becoming sociable. More like he had been at school.

Odd to see the snake charmed if not tamed. For some reason, this added to Aidan's restlessness, his sense of missing something, of *wanting* something, only he didn't know what.

He wandered around the tables at first, sipping his brandy and exchanging comments and jests with the players until he relaxed into the familiar and sat down for a game of whist.

Allowing himself only the remains of the hundred guineas he had won at the prize fight, he won often enough to keep him there.

Eventually, in a much better frame of mind, he rose with his luck about even with his losses and went upstairs to bed.

He hoped he would find Eve asleep. That way, she wouldn't notice when he slept beside her. Not that he had any intention of touching her, but he was too tall to be comfortable on the damned sofa.

He opened and closed the door softly and by the dim light of the low-burning lamp he saw that the bed was still made and untouched.

*Dear God, she's bolted.*

For an instant, he felt dizzy with panic at what accident might befall her alone in the dark. He presumed she had gone to the inn, though he doubted she had disturbed the stables for a vehicle when she had none of her own here.

He strode to the wardrobe in search of his cloak—and saw that her gowns still hung there, including the one she had worn this evening. Her hairbrush still lay on the dressing table, an unfamiliar tin of toothpowder on the washstand.

She would not bolt with nothing.

Slowly, he turned and walked forward until he saw her lying huddled on the sofa. A single blanket covered her. Her loose chestnut hair fell across her cheek.

Asleep, she looked so utterly vulnerable that his throat tightened. Something glistened on her eyelashes and her face, as though she had been weeping before sleep took her.

Guilt smote him.

But he could not leave her lying there like that while he spread himself in luxury on the bed. Bending, he slid one arm beneath her curled shape, in the vague region of her waist, and the other at the curve of her knees, and lifted her.

She stirred, making a somehow touching sound in the back of her throat, but she did not wake. The poor girl was exhausted, and no wonder.

He walked with his surprisingly light burden to the bed, and she turned her cheek into his shoulder.

There was no severity now about her face. Relaxed, her mouth was sweeter and the long eyelashes fanned against her cheeks emphasized the refined beauty of her bones. In fact, she was lovely.

Arousal stirred.

Ignoring it, he balanced some of her weight on his raised thigh, while he drew back the bedclothes with one hand. Then he laid her down gently, blanket and all, and pulled the covers over her.

He had undressed and washed before he recalled that he had brought no night shirt. It was summer after all and he had not expected company—apart from the sort that did not require clothing.

A breath of laughter caught in his throat. *Oh well.*

Leaving on his drawers for his wife's sake rather than his own, he lay down on top of the bed, and tugged the tucked in covers free to double over himself. They almost covered him.

He fell asleep with his wife's unfamiliar scent invading his senses. Oddly, he didn't mind.

# Chapter Seven

Eve woke with a start to the click of the bedroom door. Almost immediately, she recalled that she was on the sofa and realized that this must be Lord Wolf returning. On no account must she open her eyes.

She could smell his presence, warm, masculine, vital... But she could not hear him move. Was he just standing there inside the door? Why would he do that?

She risked opening her eyes and found that it was light. And that the window was in the wrong place.

Startled, she sat bolt upright. She was in the bed!

And no one else was in the room. Beside her a large, man-shaped dent in the quilt told its own story. Her whole body flamed as she realized he must have not only carried her from the sofa to the bed but lain beside her, covering himself only with what he could tug from the side of the bed.

No wonder she was too warm. She wore her robe over her nightgown and was still tangled with the spare blanket as well as all the bedclothes.

Warily, she sniffed in the vague direction of her armpit and was glad to inhale nothing too ripe.

How long would he be gone?

She had an appointment to keep with Miss Cole!

She sprang out of bed and ducked behind it to use the chamber pot. Then she ran to the washstand and went about her ablutions without actually removing her robe, so water dripped on it and on her nightgown. Then she dived into clean undergarments and her fresh morning gown.

Only then did she relax enough to wonder why she was bothered by the possibility of his return.

Reaching for her hairbrush, and stroking her way through the tugs, she stared unseeingly into the glass. Had she not dreamed of him holding her in his arms, her cheek against his warm, hard chest? Had she not half-awakened at some point to hear him breathing beside her and known sleepily that it was another foolish dream?

But it had been reality. Instead of quarrelling with her, he had made her comfortable. The intimacy she had shared with him, even unconsciously, shocked her, for though she was his wife, they were on far from intimate terms. He had already made it plain that he would touch her only for purposes of an heir and not for several years. To say nothing of the fact that he had just come from his wretched mistress!

And yet she was pathetically grateful for his kindness. Perhaps he did not hate her after all.

Or perhaps simple gentlemanly conduct, instilled in him since childhood, had won out over anger for a few minutes. And the bed was considerably more comfortable than the sofa as she had cause to know. She had slept well and deeply.

She scraped her hair back in a tight knot as usual, then paused and loosened it a little. It did actually improve her appearance, which made her feel better. At home, she had never competed with Miranda's beauty, had accepted her own plainness philosophically. Other things were of more value to her. And to Mr. Neville.

Throwing off regrets over things she could not change, she placed her final pin and rose to fetch her pelisse and hat.

Miss Cole awaited her in the hall, surrounded by three lively children. There were a boy and girl she guessed to be about ten, and a much smaller girl of about six who regarded her from unblinking, curious eyes.

"Make your bows to Lady Wolf," Miss Cole instructed them. "My lady these are my sisters, Rose and Orchid, and my cousin Alexander."

"Lily's sick," little Orchid pronounced, rather like a challenge.

"But she is on the mend," Miss Cole said firmly. She turned to Eve. "Lily being my other sister, next to me in age. Shall we go?"

"Yes!" The children ran at the front door so fast Eve almost expected them to hurl themselves against it. Instead, Alexander flung it open and they burst out into the fresh air as if they'd been catapulted.

"Do you mind them?" Harriet asked with an unexpected moment of doubt.

"Not in the least. I like children."

"Some people do mind. But we are all used to being together, and it irks them—and me, if I am strictly honest—that propriety compels us to be so much apart under the same roof. Do you have brothers and sisters of your own?"

"Just one sister who is only two years younger than myself. But I have a few little cousins. And the orphans, of course."

Miss Cole was commendably interested in the orphans, and while they struck out from the garden over the meadow, and the children ran around them, dashing backwards and forwards, the adult ladies entertained each other with tales of funny childish antics.

As they paused on a stile to rest, it came to Eve that Miss Cole had not once treated her as anything other than an equal. She had even invited her to use her Christian name.

While the children were rushing around picking daisies to make a necklaces with, Harriet grew silent.

"Is something troubling you?" Eve asked, hoping it was not herself.

Harriet cast her a quick, rueful smile. "I am wondering whether or not to tell you something that is none of my business and might offend you."

"Well, you'll have to tell me now or I'll be eaten up with anxiety. I assure you, I am very thick-skinned."

Harriet's eyes were shrewd. "I don't think you are. But I'll say it anyway because I have this idea it might make you feel better." She took a breath, as if for courage. "I think you have probably heard the rumours about your husband and Mrs. Archer. I have no idea whether or not they are true, but like you, I saw them enter the drawing room after the gentlemen last night, not quite together. Gossips will draw their own conclusions and there's nothing you can do about that. But I was talking to Lord Sanderly..." She flushed slightly. "You know we are betrothed? Well, we talk of many things when we are alone, and he told me Lord Wolf left the dining room only when he and all the other gentlemen did, and that Lord Wolf could only have exchanged the briefest word with Mrs. Archer before they entered the drawing room."

Eve dropped her eyes, realized she had torn up a handful of grass, and tossed it away.

"Thank you for explaining to me," she said with difficulty. "But please don't be concerned. It does not matter. Our marriage is one of convenience, not of deeper feelings that can be hurt."

"Oh, feelings can always be hurt," Harriet said vaguely. She rose and jumped down from the step, calling for the children.

AIDAN, GLAD TO WAKE before his wife and avoid her outrage at his daring to sleep beside her, had dressed silently in riding clothes and crept from his own room like an illicit lover, clutching his boots in his hand.

He sat on the stairs to put them on, then left the house with some relief at encountering no one, and took Atlas, his horse of whom he was inordinately fond, for a long ride and an intimate chat.

Aidan was not given to introspection, but he did not much like the man who emerged from his conversation with Atlas.

He had been quick enough to grab Romilly's money and yet had not treated his wife with any human consideration, nursing his own outrage at trickery rather than actually *thinking*. What the devil would he have done if he had read the agreement properly and known the price was marriage?

Walked away? Thrown himself on the non-existent mercy of Wilsborough and the others and pleaded for time? Abandoned Patrick to the opprobrium of his peers for welching on a debt of honour? Watched his struggling estate go under with all his people?

No, he would always have taken the money and paid the price. And now he was behaving like a petulant child.

Atlas did not disagree with him.

"I suppose there are other aspects of my life that could bear some scrutiny," he said to the horse.

Atlas twitched one ear.

"Am I an unprincipled rake?"

Atlas shook his head and reached for the succulent leaves hanging over the lane. Firmly, Aidan tightened the reins again and faced the horse forward.

"I am just like you grabbing the leaves, thoughtlessly making the most of my opportunities. I was glad to find Helena here, even with her weaselly husband. I'm fond of her and she is a luscious lover. But in truth she might as well be Daisy the opera dancer or Tilda from the Black Horse inn."

That was not respectful or kind to either Helena or any of the other casual mistresses he had known over the years. It certainly did not consider Archer, who might be an unpleasant human being, but still, when Aidan considered what his own feelings might be if *his* wife took a lover...

"It's no use telling myself I haven't touched Helena since coming to Grand Court," he told the horse ruefully. "The intent was there. I don't like Archer. Helena doesn't like him. Not sure that's a good enough excuse. After all, Eve doesn't like me." He scowled at the horse. "Damn it, Atlas, I'm not even sure I like Helena. Not beyond the physical delights anyway… The *really* odd thing is, I might like Eve if I could stop quarrelling with her for long enough. Or digging her out of whatever stupid holes she keeps casting herself—or me! —into. Oh the devil, let's gallop."

Things definitely clarified in his mind as he turned Atlas's head back toward Grand Court. And the sight of Helena herself, mounted in the midst of a small group of riders setting out on a hack across the meadow, confirmed not just his duty but his preference.

He could not speak to her in company, and he would not cause gossip by detaching her from the others. So he merely passed them at a distance with a wave and shouted, "Good morning!"

However, Atlas was tired after his gallop, and their slow walk meant that it was easy for Helena to catch up with him.

"Changed your mind?" he asked, surprised.

"The company was too dull for words. I'm sure Grand Court parties used to be much more amusing. Rushing back to the little wife, Aidan? Or have you been avoiding her all morning?"

The latter guess was all too close to the mark and her smile told him she knew it. As they crested the rise in the meadow, Grand Court's formal, terraced gardens spread out before them.

The garden was largely empty of the usual strollers and flirting couples, since most of Lady Grandison's guests were no doubt spending a leisurely day in anticipation of the evening's ball. But at one corner Aidan made out a few running children, chasing each other along paths and up and down steps, dodging around flower beds and fountains, statues and benches in what was clearly an energetic and hilarious game of tag. Their laughter drifted on the wind, a sound of pure, innocent jollity, an echo of half-forgotten childhood fun.

Aidan could not help smiling. "Miss Cole's family." He could even see Harriet herself, lounging on a stone seat.

"Look again," Helena drawled.

She was right. Unless the sick sister had recovered dramatically, there were too many girls scampering around that rose bush. One of them was tall enough to be an adult. A very slender, shapely woman who darted suddenly down the terrace steps with a small boy pelting after her.

It could only be Eve. He almost laughed, only Helena was speaking once more.

"I thought you would like to see for yourself and explain to her. She really has no idea how to go on among civilised people."

That was why Helena had followed him. She had really thought he would be repelled, angry, and ashamed. From sheer malice she had wanted to watch his reactions.

Deliberately, he turned to face her, leaving the smile on his lips. "You would have cut her last night. Understand I do not tolerate such *civilised* behaviour. You must excuse me. I am off to play tag."

And he urged poor Atlas to a canter, leaving Helena with her mouth agape.

EVE DID NOT KNOW HOW long the watchers on the hill had been there before she noticed them. But she recognized her husband at once, just from his somehow lazy poise in the saddle. And she certainly knew Mrs. Archer from her dashing scarlet riding habit, for Eve, Harriet and the children had returned from their walk via the path to the stables and met the group of riders just starting out. At the time, she had felt foolishly glad that Lord Wolf was not among them.

Now they were alone together and watching her dash around like a hoyden with someone else's children.

"Tag!" Alexander yelled in triumph, poking her in the back.

Forcing herself, Eve leapt after him, then suddenly changed paths and went after Orchid, who squealed, and dashed behind the fountain.

Eve chased her round it for a bit, then swerved to catch Rose, laughing at the edge of the path.

"Tag!"

The game went on, though Eve's heart was no longer in it. After a little, she bowed out and went instead to sit beside Harriet.

"Thank you," Harriet said. "It's my aim to exhaust them without exhausting myself so that they don't cause havoc at the ball tonight. But I hope you haven't used up all the energy you will need for dancing."

Eve smiled distractedly. "I shan't be dancing. Oh dear." The last came as she spotted the familiar figure of Lord Wolf striding around from the direction of the stables. Hastily, she stood up. "I should see what I can do to make my gown more suitable. Excuse me."

She hurried away in the direction of the house, with an airy wave to the children, pretending she saw neither the approach of her husband nor the frown of incomprehension on Harriet's brow.

She despised herself for a craven coward, but she was not ready yet to face Lord Wolf. She did not want to resume the quarrel over her approach to Mrs. Archer last night, which had clearly made him feel humiliated and foolish in some way. Besides which, she had given the woman the opportunity to cut her. Eve was loweringly aware that many others would take their lead from the gently born woman they knew rather than the encroaching cit's daughter who had dared to marry above her station. At the very least, it was fuel for gossip, and Eve did recognize that Wolf's intervention was timely.

She would not have minded humbly admitting that fact. It might avert another quarrel. Only there was still the Matter of The Bed. He had carried her there. He had lain beside her. It all made her hot and uncomfortable and she had no idea how to meet him now.

And yet they needed to talk before the day wore on too far. She had agreed to stay for the ball because it would cause less talk. But that was before her faux pas of approaching Mrs. Archer. He might well prefer now that she leave before the ball, and if she was to reach Wolverton Hall before the middle of the night, she would have to set off very soon.

Could a post-chaise be ordered from the village inn? Or a vehicle borrowed?

Although her instinct was to avoid it, she decided to return to Wolf's bedchamber, and so scurried past the breakfast parlour from where a pleasant hum of chatter now emanated. She smiled with vague amiability and inclined her head to two ladies on the stairs. They returned the greeting civilly but did not linger.

Safe in the bedchamber, she did not know what to do with herself. She could not simply pace the floor or sit gazing into space until he came in to change out of his riding clothes. This might not happen for hours, for he was probably with Mrs. Archer...

The thought propelled her to the wardrobe where her gowns were hung alongside her husband's two coats, two pairs of pantaloons and one pair of black silk knee breeches. Either he travelled light or his clothing budget was modest. She was sure that Patrick Wolf wore newer garments.

But that was not her concern. She took down the evening dress she had not yet worn and spread it on the bed while she examined it dubiously. It was pretty in an unassuming kind of way, suitable for dinner or even the theatre but much too plain for a ball.

She glanced at the gown she had worn last night, and then at her spare day dress. She would not need either of those if they were leaving tomorrow. Then she recalled the extravagant diamond-headed hairpins that her father had given her on her eighteenth birthday. She had never worn them, though Miranda had. Eve had meant to give them to her sister as a long-term loan when they met in London.

The germ of an idea began to grow, and she seized upon it with desperation.

By the time Lord Wolf walked into his chamber, she had made tatters of the other dresses, removing the trims, and had scattered everything over the bed. She sat cross-legged among the carnage, attaching lace to the bodice and hem of her one intact evening gown.

He paused on the threshold and she glanced up guiltily.

"What the devil are you doing?" He closed the door and strode in. "Is this temper, my lady? Don't you know my purse will not stretch to the replacing of such destruction?"

"Mine will," she said unwisely. She meant only that he need not feel responsible for dressing her but the angry flush staining his cheekbones told her she'd been tactless.

"Yet another point that need not be laboured. I am aware of your superior wealth, though I cannot imagine your father earned it by such acts of wanton waste."

"I d-do not have a ballgown," she said, stammering slightly. "I thought I could make this one more suitable."

"It doesn't matter what you look like," he said impatiently.

That was true, and it shouldn't have hurt to hear the words. "I will be less visible in a more suitable gown. But you are probably right that I shouldn't bother. What do you want me to do?"

"Do?" He threw the question over his shoulder as he strode on to the desk.

"I thought you might have changed your mind about my attending the ball."

He threw himself into the chair and drew writing materials toward himself. "Of course not."

And that appeared to be that. She dragged her gaze free of him and returned to her sewing. Clearly, he did not wish to be interrupted.

He wrote and she sewed in silence for some five minutes, after which he sanded his letter, folded it and sealed it with the ring on his finger.

"If you have your letter," he said rising, "I will drop it at the inn with my own."

"Letter?" she repeated momentarily confused. Dear God, had she forgotten all about the orphans in her own feeble troubles? She dropped everything and scrambled off the bed.

"Give me one moment, if you please," she managed.

"I am at your disposal," he said glacially. "Unless you have changed your mind about my spare house?"

"I have not," she muttered.

*My dear Mr. Neville,* she wrote in haste. Suddenly she felt quite overcome by the sadness of writing to him while married to another man. She would even have to sign it *Eve Wolf*, not *Romilly*, or even simply *Eve* for that would not be proper for a married lady.

Brushing such inanities aside, she wrote starkly of Lord Wolf's offer of the use of his house for the orphanage, and informed Mr. Neville that his lordship's man of business would contact him very soon on the subject.

Then she scribbled his name and direction on the folded letter and passed it to her husband unsealed.

He didn't take it. "I shan't read it, you know. You may feel free to write your tender goodbyes."

She didn't know if he was warning her or mocking her. Either way, she could think of no reply. After a moment's silence he merely took the letter from her and sealed it himself.

"Dinner will be early and informal tonight, but I shall be back before then." And then he was gone again.

# Chapter Eight

Helena Archer sat in the window seat of the garden room, watching a sudden shower of rain splash down the glass and obliterate the pleasant gardens from view. After several days of fine weather, it seemed the skies were not prepared to cooperate with Lady Grandison's plans to allow the ball to spill outdoors.

Tea had been served in the garden salon before most people had drifted off again, leaving only Helena and Mrs. Alicia Eldridge in the room. Helena did not really have friends—she had people who amused her or who were useful to her—but there was a kind of shallow understanding between the two women. Once or twice, for their own entertainment, they had even competed for the same lover and wagered on the outcome.

Alicia had won the last wager, for Lord Sanderly, some months ago, much to Helena's irritation for she had had to hand over her favourite bracelet. There was, besides, something about the man's ruthless remoteness from his fellow human beings that intrigued her. She grumbled that it was easier for Alicia, being widowed, than for Helena who had to practise at least some discretion in the vicinity of her husband.

Annoyingly, Alicia had been inclined to gloat, hinting at the unique pleasures to be found in her new lover, however much of a pariah he was to Society. However, the liaison had clearly not lasted. Sanderly had not gone near her for months. She had harboured brief hopes of reviving the affair at Grand Court after his unexpected arrival, and at first he *had* seemed inclined to flirt—or at least what passed for flirting in Sanderly. Only he'd then changed his mind to pursue Lady Grandison's goddaughter instead.

"I wish him joy of his ingenue," Alicia said abruptly from the next window seat.

Helena cast her a cynical smile. "Wait until he's married her, my dear. I'm sure boredom if nothing else will send him scurrying back to your charms. What can she offer him, after all?"

Alicia did not appear to like that idea. "Is that your best hope for Wolf?" she snapped.

"The situations are quite different," Helena retorted. "Wolf married for money. Any fool could see he was appalled that she followed him here. Why else would he have told no one of her existence? There was not even an announcement in the newspapers."

"Then you think he is bored already?" Alicia asked, apparently amused. "She might be too quiet and a shade awkward, but she *is* rather beautiful, in an uncommon kind of a way."

"In a virginal kind of a way," Helena corrected with a curl of her lips. "If he has bedded her, I'll eat my new hat. She has merely spoiled his sport." *And mine.*

"For a short time only, I'm sure," Alicia said with more sympathy.

Helena was not so sure. Cutting the under-bred girl who had dared to buy Wolf had seemed so amusing and satisfying last night, even though he had rescued his wife at the last possible second. She was surprised at the time that he had troubled to intervene, for her ladyship's absence from Society could only benefit him. But Helena was forced to acknowledge her mistake. She had played a bad hand and forced him to choose.

And being honourable, damn him, he had chosen his wife.

Rather than seeing the funny side, he had turned against Helena and she knew in her heart she would never get him back. That hurt.

"Did you love him then?" Alicia asked.

"I am not so foolish. Or ridiculous." Wasn't she? It had begun as mere sport but there was something about Wolf's whole-hearted focus on her pleasure, combined with his careless, good-natured charm, that was utterly disarming, utterly...

"Addictive," Alicia said ruefully. "Like Sanderly, in his own way. What we need to lift our spirits, my dear, is a spot of revenge. Then we shall both move on to another, more difficult wager. What about the Duke of Death?"

Helena raised her brows. "You mean he's still alive? I've never set eyes on the man."

"You probably have, you just didn't realize it. But yes, we shall have to hurry before the poor boy turns up his toes."

"Right now, I'm more interested in the revenge. What had you in mind? Something petty and truly hurtful, I hope?"

"So do I," Alicia said dreamily. "Though it should not rule out future possibilities for our misguided lovers. It is, in fact, quite amusing and terribly, terribly simple..."

AIDAN HAD WALKED INTO the village at a brisk pace, which was thirsty work under the warm sunshine. Having dropped his letters into the Royal Mail sack at the inn, he sat down in the tap room with a pint of ale. And then, since he would miss luncheon at Grand Court, he ordered a quick meal.

He was not particularly looking forward to the evening's ball. Responsibilities to his wife loomed too large. He did not put it past Helena to spread some poison that would isolate Eve, depriving her of dance partners and companionship, so he would have to look after her and, if necessary, kick some of his friends into doing the pretty.

No, he had little anticipation of enjoyment. He was actually looking forward to leaving and going home where he would no longer need to worry about his wife. Which was stupid, really. He had come here to escape her and everything associated with her. Now he was escaping from here and the chaos she had brought with her.

Not that he was blameless. He had behaved ill and made a bad situation worse. Time to go home and reach some kind of equilibrium that they could both live with. He could set in motion the repairs around the estate that he had earmarked Romilly's extra two thousand for and decide how best to spend the rest of it.

The question of his wife's maintenance bothered him. It was something he had never discussed with Romilly, for he had been far too angry at the time, but it had certainly exploded into his head when he saw her expensive gowns lying in pieces all over her bed. Such wanton destruction had incensed him as well as scared him, but of course he had been wrong about that too.

Dress and strict propriety meant little to him, but she had forced him to acknowledge that unsuitable dress would make her a laughingstock at least to some degree. Though God knew what sort of ludicrous patchwork garment she was going to come up with. Perhaps he had been wrong to force her to stay.

*Oh well...*

He should clear the air with her, too. Somehow, he did not want her to be in continued receipt of an allowance from her father—it was a husband's business to maintain his wife and family. And yet Aidan could not keep her in decent clothing. Not after he had paid for Patrick's, shelled out to the rest of the family pensioners, *and* paid his annual dues to Romilly.

Well, Patrick would have to tighten his damned belt. It was his extravagance that had caused this mess, and it was time he did more for the family fortunes than merely rusticate for a few months of the year.

Draining the last of his ale, he rose and paid his shot and walked out. The sky had clouded over a bit, an ill omen for Lady Grandison's ball.

An ill-dressed, vaguely familiar young man limped toward him. Aidan, with too much on his mind to be bothered to think how he knew the fellow, merely nodded curtly and received the same gesture in return.

He arrived back at Grand Court just before the heavens opened and in perfect time for tea. At some point before the party broke up, he realized his wife was not present. He hoped she was not going to be a clingy creature, refusing to go anywhere without him…

Damn it, she had come here without him and had planned to go to London by herself afterward. She was a capable, independent woman, and he would have to get out of the habit of looking for the worst in her. Why did he do that?

Excusing himself to his companions, he repaired to his bedchamber. Where his mouth fell open in shock.

Eve stood before the glass, an expression of doubt on her really rather lovely face. Her hair had come half-loose from its pins and tumbled about her face and shoulders on one side. A beam of late afternoon sun shone through the window, making her hair gleam and the skin of her neck and breast glow. The unusual, old-gold shade of the evening gown he had once thought dull, contrasted with an ivory gauze overdress that hung in glittering folds from her shoulders to calves, open at the front to reveal the high-waisted, low-necked lace bodice.

She looked ethereal and lovely, like some fairytale princess.

Apart from the way she bit her lip, and the half-frightened, half-despairing look she cast at him.

"I think I spoiled those dresses for nothing. Perhaps Miss Cole could lend me something…"

"Miss Cole is several inches shorter than you," Aidan said, still staring. "Did you achieve all of that yourself?"

"I was always a decent needlewoman, but Papa would not let me make my own gowns, even for every day."

"No reason why you should work your fingers to the bone, but I have to say the effect is stunning. What is it that is glittering? Are those *diamonds*?" He strode up to her to find out. "Where on earth did they come from?"

She blushed. "They're hair pins I was going to give to my sister."

He blinked. "*Hair pins*? Won't they scratch you to ribbons and make you bleed?"

"No, I blunted them and wound thread around them when I sewed them from the gauze to the main gown. Do I look too ridiculous?"

He licked his dry lips. "No. No, you look lovely. Unique and perfect."

She peered at him as though looking for the mockery.

Impatiently, he took her by the shoulders and turned her back toward the glass. "Look. The dress is a work of art, but that is not your beauty."

She laughed. "*I* have none of that. Though I thank you for the flatt—"

"Who says so?" he interrupted.

"I am not blind," she said tartly.

"Yes, you are," he muttered, for he had begun to suspect *he* was too. He had not wanted anything about her to be good or pleasant in any way because he'd needed every grievance to keep his anger alive. He met her gaze in the glass. "I'm sorry. I have behaved ill since we met. I don't find it easy to be a supplicant. I know our marriage has destroyed the lives we each hoped for, yours far more than mine, and yet you are the innocent party."

Her gaze dropped as though she were embarrassed, and she made to turn away from him. But he tightened his fingers on her tense, delicate shoulders, keeping her in place and her eyes flew back to his.

"Our lives need not be ruined," he said. "We did not choose each other but we can deal better together. We can be better friends, if nothing else."

A frown flickered across her brow. She swallowed. "I would like us to be friends. I would like us to be comfortable."

"Then we have an agreement of our own." He dropped his arms to his sides, and she seemed to breathe again. "In the absence of a lady's maid, may I help you out of this delightful garment before dinner?"

Her eyes widened. "If you would not mind just unfastening the first three hooks, I can manage."

"How on earth did you fasten them in the first place?" he asked, obeying her. She had a rather beautiful nape, long and slender.

"With some ungainly contortions, but I'm not sure the gown will stand much more of that."

Amused, he reached down to gather the fine layers of the gown in his hands, and she whisked herself away like a startled kitten. From instinct, he flirted and teased.

"Don't be shy, wife of my bosom. Recall that you slept beside my naked body for most of the night."

Her face flamed. Even her shoulders and breast seemed to turn pink. "N-naked?" she stammered.

"I had no nightshirt, and I am too long to stretch out on so short a sofa. Now stop being missish and let me help."

This time, she stayed still while he carefully drew the gown up and over her head, leaving her touchingly vulnerable in her chemise. From sheer embarrassment no doubt, she breathed too rapidly, and while he obligingly hung up her ballgown, she hastily flung on her own morning gown.

"Allow me," he said politely. "Longing as I am to witness said contortions, I am at heart a gentleman." Her doubtful gaze met his in the glass once more and he grinned at her and rather valued the way her face relaxed into a shy smile as she realized they were sharing a joke.

LORD WOLF'S SMILE WAS a stunning revelation. He had never smiled at her like that before, as if he had meant it. The corners of his eyes crinkled, while his eyes themselves seemed to dance. His sensual mouth curved upward and his whole face lit up. He was dazzling.

And she, his plain, unloved wife, was lost.

To cover her confusion, as soon as he had fastened the gown for her, she hastily gathered up her hair and repaired the half-fallen knot behind her head.

"I thought for the ball, I could weave the pearl necklace through it," she said nervously. *Why did I speak? He cannot possibly be interested in such trivia.*

"Good idea," he said, removing his coat and cravat. "I'll help."

Eve did not immediately respond, for he had just tugged his shirt up over his head and her breath vanished altogether. Dear God, he was beautiful, all muscle and sinew rippling beneath his golden skin. Her mouth went dry. She longed to touch him.

Shocked, she spun away, hopefully before he saw her staring like a starving woman at a beef steak. What was the matter with her?

*Is this love, then? Not the gentle friendship and understanding of shared values that I felt for Mr. Neville, but this wild, physical longing for... For what?*

*Idiot. A moment of madness is not love.*

*Thank God.* For what could be worse than loving the husband who had to steel himself to be kind to his despised wife?

Why could she not feel the same gentle friendship with *him*? Every feeling seemed too intense, too raw, too...

"Have you seen much of the house yet?" he asked. "Grandison has a rather fine library if you are interested in books?"

"I am," she said, grasping this neutral topic like a lifeline. "I should like to see it."

The time until dinner passed very pleasantly, at first alone with her husband in the library, discovering fascinating books and reading little snatches from them. She had the impression she had surprised Lord Wolf by the breadth and depth of her interests, but then he rather surprised her by his knowledge too. He was, it seemed, rather more than the careless if charming hedonist she had imagined him.

She thought back to her solitary days at Wolverton Hall and realized that none of the tenants had spoken of their landlord with anything but liking and respect.

A little later, they were joined by Sir Ralph Lawrence, a local member of parliament, and by an older gentleman called Mr. Thornton who reminded her a little of Mr. Neville. They proved agreeable company. To her surprise, both of them asked her to save dances for them, and although she knew they asked through respect for Lord Wolf, she appreciated the gesture and was glad she would not have the embarrassment of sitting out every dance. She was too used to playing the wallflower to Miranda's beauty to hope for miracles, but the truth was, she loved dancing.

They all went through to a light buffet dinner together, and Eve's stomach rumbled embarrassingly. Fortunately, she only happened to be with Lord Wolf at the time, and his eyes gleamed with laughter.

"Sorry," she whispered. "I've just realized this is the first time I've eaten today! No wonder I'm hungry."

He did not look quite so amused by this, but he gave no response, presumably realizing she had been busy with the ballgown all day.

Dinner was enlivened by the presence of guests from elsewhere in the county, some of whom were already in their ball finery. Eve was introduced to several of them, though she could not afterwards remember most of their names—which was unfortunate since she promised dances to at least two. But, encouragingly, she would not embarrass her husband by being too noted a wallflower, and she could certainly enjoy the dancing. Perhaps tonight would not be so bad after all.

The very thought must have tempted providence.

# Chapter Nine

It began well. When she entered the ballroom on her husband's arm, a few heads turned but she intercepted no obvious stares of contempt.

*They've got used to me*, she thought optimistically. And perhaps Wolf was right that the altered gown worked for her. She thought it more likely that his magic with her hair distracted attention. This time she had let herself enjoy the sensation of his fingers moving over her sensitive skin, threading the pearl necklace through the elegant knot pinned high on her head, from where one thick sleek rope of hair fell to her shoulder, just nestling at her collar bone.

"I would never have thought of that," she had told him in wonder.

"I had the idea when I first saw you in the dress and some of your hair had come loose."

It was, of course, marvellous that he should take such pains with her. It was equally important that her appearance, over which she had never laboured before, did not let him down. She had to at least look the part of a baroness.

And she began to hope that between them, they had managed that first hurdle. Lady Grandison smiled at her with kind approval. Her husband, Sir John gently squeezed her gloved fingers and told her she looked charming.

Lady Bab Martindale rustled over to them almost at once. "I love your gown," she said with what appeared to be genuine envy. "You must give me the name of your dressmaker."

The ballroom, already lit by chandeliers even though it was not yet quite dark, and decorated with a riot of fresh flowers and young orange trees in pots, smelled a little like a hothouse. But since the rain had obligingly vanished, a pleasant draught of air circulated from the open glass doors to the terrace. The exquisite scents of the summer flowers drifted in the air.

It felt almost magical, particularly when, as soon as the music began, Mr. Martindale invited her to dance. Eve began to enjoy herself. She had no time even to sit down afterward for she was claimed by Lord Sanderly. Thoroughly happy to be dancing, she did not mind at all that both gentlemen were clearly obliging their friend, Lord Wolf.

More surprising was the honour of being chosen by their host, Sir John Grandison. "Very glad of the chance to make your acquaintance properly," he said kindly as he led her into the set. "You must notice everyone's curiosity to meet the lady who finally tamed the Wolf!"

"Oh, I wouldn't," she said seriously. "Everyone seems to like him as he is."

Sir John's lips twitched. "A novel approach for a bride."

"Well, I am practical. I could not change him if I wanted to."

"He is a good man," Sir John said, "as well as excellent company."

That gave her a pang, because although she had indeed enjoyed the merest taste of his company, she knew that was all he would ever bestow upon her. He did not love her and never would, because that twelve thousand pounds would come between them more surely than other women like Mrs. Archer.

The dance parted them and brought them back to turn together.

"And whatever rumours you may hear, despite being no saint, he was never *rakishly* inclined," Sir John murmured. "In fact, I always thought him a little lonely."

This was such a novel view of her popular husband that she danced in silence, mulling it over.

Aristocrats on the verge of poverty married money. Lord Wolf never had until Patrick forced the issue, although in all probability he'd known he would have to eventually. He had not the luxury of falling in love and choosing a poor bride. And so he probably eased his loneliness with unattainable women like Mrs. Archer, or with others who did not or could not expect marriage. A form of defence, a guarding of his heart while finding only the semblance of true human contact. His genuine feeling all went into friendships. Men liked him for that reason. Women liked him, probably, for the challenge of touching his heart.

And this was all pure speculation which achieved nothing. She could most help him—and herself—by enjoying the evening and being agreeable to those friends.

She danced with Sir Ralph Lawrence, and a young man whose name she had forgotten, and by then realized with awe that at least as far as partners were concerned, this was her most successful dance ever. Miranda, her father, and her aunt, would be stunned. It seemed there were some benefits to being a baroness.

Best of all, she had just parted from the nameless young man to make her way back to her seat—she had decided to sit out the upcoming waltz and rest—when she almost bumped into her husband.

It was so unexpected—since the ball had opened, she had only laid eyes on him over a distance—and she was so pleased to see him, that she smiled without reserve.

He seemed surprised, too. Certainly, his breath hitched before he said lightly, "At last. The lady in demand."

"Everyone has been so kind!"

"Is that what you think? Is it kindness if I ask you to waltz with me?"

"Well, no, for husbands and wives are not meant to dance with each other, are they? Besides, I have never waltzed with a man before."

He blinked. "With a horse?"

She laughed at the ridiculous image. "With my sister." Miranda had thought the dance was fast, so naturally she had wanted to learn.

"Perhaps you would risk it with a mere husband? Since we are newly married, I daresay the arbiters of fashion might forgive us."

She peered at him. "Are you serious?"

"Rarely. I see I shall have to invoke husbandly authority." He offered his arm.

With a funny little twinge of anticipation, she laid her hand upon it.

Few unmarried girls had taken to the floor, although Harriet Cole was there with Lord Sanderly. Most of the other women were smart young matrons like Mrs. Archer.

Eve actually jumped when Wolf took her into his arms. Inexplicably shocked, her eyes flew up to his.

"Too grim?" he asked ruefully.

She shook her head, lost for words. In truth she felt overwhelmed, especially once the dancing began and she had to pay such attention to the movements of his body. Following his lead was easy, novel, and then exhilarating, for although they were so close, they barely touched except in the clasp of their hands, which was usual enough. Admittedly there was the circle of his arm at her back but that was light, respectful. The hardest seemed to be her fingers on his shoulder for if she slid her hand just a little higher it would be around his neck…

She was afraid nerves at such intimacy would make her stumble, but in fact, focusing on the steps and the rhythm distracted her until she relaxed and found the courage to say what had to be said.

"Your words this afternoon were gracious and kind," she blurted. "I need to tell you that there is much I regret, too. Not least my own temper. I did come to beg the use of your house for the orphanage, but also, I meant to punish you for what I perceived as your rudeness to me."

"You had some cause," he allowed. "I'm not surprised you despise me."

"I don't. I never did. That is the other thing I need to tell you. Before we can really begin again as friends."

She could not quite read his expression.

"It is you who are gracious," he said, and turned just a little too fast.

With the air cleared of her most immediate anxieties, she relaxed further and, it seemed, so did he, for by the end of the dance they were bantering, and her heart was so full she felt it might explode.

Oh yes, she loved him. And more than that, there might even be hope for their friendship. She had no right to ache for more.

AIDAN'S WIFE WAS PROVING to be something of a revelation tonight. Her spontaneous smile when they had met had been unexpectedly dazzling, the admission that she did not truly despise him surprisingly welcome. He was learning that there were layers to her. Even if her efforts at rapprochement were merely to make her own life easier, he could hardly blame her for that. If they both tried, he might even enjoy having her in his life.

It would have been too gauche to give into his impulse to keep her for the supper dance too, so he let her go with a bow, and deliberately turned away rather than watch her go.

"Help me out, Wolf," Mrs. Eldridge said, taking his arm. "Pretend we are engaged for the supper dance or I will be obliged to spend the next hour or more with Wriggley. The boy has hands everywhere."

"Shall I have a word?" Aidan asked frowning, for although Mrs. Eldridge was hardly a close friend, she was a widow and his chivalrous instincts were aroused. A woman was entitled not to be mauled. Besides, she had once been connected to Snake, whom he counted a friend.

"No, no, just protect me with your presence! Don't worry, you need not actually dance with me. Would you care for a breath of air instead?"

"Actually, I would."

They walked together toward the open French doors to the torch-lit terrace and the garden beyond, whose main paths were prettily lit with lanterns. The fresher air was pleasant on his skin, the mild breeze stirring his hair very welcome. Since the supper dance was beginning, the terrace was quiet.

"I'm afraid you must forgive my subterfuge," Mrs. Eldridge said. "I was afraid if I did not appeal to your chivalry you would not come. And someone needs a word with you very badly."

*Damnation, I walked into that one.* As Mrs. Eldridge released his arm and flitted away, Helena emerged from the shadows.

He turned abruptly back toward the house.

"Don't go," she pleaded. "I do need to talk to you. I need to apologize and know we are friends, so that I might have the strength to move on."

He paused, for he had never heard her so serious. Uneasily, he began to wonder if her heart had been more engaged in their affair than he had assumed.

Guiltily, now, he turned back to face her. "There is no need to apologize. We had fun, Helena, and I will always remember you fondly."

"Then you do not hate me for my jealousy?"

In his mind he had called it spite. Fresh shame twinged. "I could never hate you. But my duty is to protect my wife."

"I understand," she said with a humility he had never heard in her before. "Would my own husband had a fraction of your proper feeling."

"I'm sorry, Helena. I know things are difficult for you. I...I do wish you happiness."

"It just can't be with you, can it?" she said sadly.

He shook his head and she thrust out her hand. He took it. They stood thus in silence for a few moments. He had owed her more than simply riding away from her as he had this afternoon, and he hadn't even known it.

She raised sorrowful eyes to his face. He remembered how beautiful he had once thought her. Her fingers clung to his.

"Then let us kiss and part," she whispered, stepping hesitantly closer. Her eyes flickered over his shoulder, as though making sure they were still alone.

Aidan did not really want to kiss her, but it was easy and familiar. The strength of her response took him by surprise. For several moments, she plastered herself to him, her arms tight around his neck, her mouth fused to his.

Eventually, he reached up to break her hold on his neck, but she released him quite suddenly.

"Thank you," she said fervently. "Goodbye, Aidan."

He found himself scratching his head as he watched her retreat into the ballroom. Foolishly, he had once imagined that he knew women, but it seemed now that he would never understand them.

EVE SAT IN HER QUIET corner, actually glad to be alone when Harriet skipped off with Sir Ralph for the supper dance. She still felt confused, almost dreamy, after her waltz with her husband. She guessed she would not have many such memories and so she wanted to savour it, to recall every touch, every word, and then store it all away for the difficult times when pain and loneliness might eat her up.

*I will be his friend, and I will make him comfortable. He will never know.*

"Lady Wolf?"

Eve blinked.

Mrs. Eldridge, the beautiful widow, stood before her, smiling. "I am the bearer of a most secret message," she said, dropping into the empty chair next to her. She lowered her voice, her eyes dancing with fun. "Your husband requests a most unfashionable assignation with his lady, out on the terrace. Don't tell anyone!"

And she swept away again. Eve, who half-expected it was a trick to make fun of her, rose and walked casually to the terrace door. The fact that Mrs. Eldridge walked in the other direction gave her hope that the message was genuine.

She slipped outside and glanced to left and right—and there stood a couple in a most passionate embrace. The torchlight glared down on his fine, handsome features. It was quite clearly her husband, kissing Mrs. Archer.

Only the pain of her own fingers digging into the skin over her heart enabled her to jerk away from the unbearable sight. And yet she should have expected this. It was a taste of her future, now that she had learned to care.

Blindly, she walked back into the ballroom, pride plastering a faint smile to her lips, a smile she could not maintain. She had done her duty for the day and could bear no more.

She skirted the dance floor, unaware with whom she exchanged nods, and climbed the stairs to the main part of the house. The front hall still blazed with light, although it was blessedly empty. She climbed the staircase, past the first landing where she could hear someone moving about, and on up to the floor above. She turned into the passage, refusing to give in to her stupid weakness before she reached his room.

*This time, I will stay awake until we leave... By then I will have risen above my own idiocy. I* will...

She opened the door and went in.

A man bent over the chest of drawers from which he appeared to be throwing things to the floor. He straightened and stared at her.

She stopped dead. "Who are you? What on earth are you doing?"

And then blinding pain crashed into her head and she was falling through a whirlpool of dizzying darkness.

A rough, aggrieved voice from a great distance demanded, "What did you do that for, numbskull?"

"She was about to scream," said another at a much lower pitch. "Besides, look at her, she's got diamonds all over her."

Something tugged at her. She could not even whimper, let alone scream.

The lower voice swore. "Take her with us."

"Jonty'll kill you!"

"Not with all these diamonds, he won't. Besides, she ain't dead yet, but she might well be by the time anyone finds her. If we don't want to hang, we take her to a doctor."

"Oh, aye, it'll do her the world of good to be thrown out of a window and bumped over a saddle!"

When she drew in her breath to scream, agony sliced through her brain and the world went completely silent.

AIDAN FELT RATHER GRUBBY after his encounter with Helena, so he did not at once look for his wife. He presumed she was dancing and was glad for her sake. Only as everyone went in to supper did Harriet and Snake stop him.

"Where is Eve?" Harriet asked. "We agreed to have supper together."

"Wasn't she dancing?"

"No, she sat it out."

Aidan looked about him and stopped Sir Ralph Lawrence. "I don't suppose you've seen my wife?"

"She left the ballroom a while ago. I didn't see her come back."

"I'll go to the cloakroom and make sure she's well," Harriet said.

For some reason, Aidan felt uneasy, which was foolish. At least Harriet was not long, although she returned alone.

"The hall footman saw her go upstairs. I think she has gone to bed."

Aidan blinked, annoyance rising to the fore. "In the middle of the ball? Was she ill?"

"The footman did not think so."

*Damn the woman, doesn't she know how rude she's being? Can she not behave properly for one wretched evening?* Even as the thought rushed through his brain, he was aware of how ridiculous it was. That *he* should reproach anyone for—or even notice—improper behaviour!

After all, he had just let his ex-mistress kiss him.

Awareness of his own shortcomings only fed his wrath. "Give my apologies to Lady Grandison if I don't come back," he said curtly to Snake and strode out of the ballroom and upstairs.

On the first floor landing, he heard sounds coming from the dimly lit gallery. Which was odd. No one had reason to be there just now. The servants were all busy with the ball. On impulse, he went to investigate and pushed open the drawing room door.

A lantern lay on one of the exquisite marquetry tables. By its light, an ill-dressed man was throwing things out an open window.

*Burglary!*

Outraged, he was about to stride across the room when he froze in sudden blinding fear.

*Eve.*

If there were others, if she had encountered them… He could not risk being delayed by a fight with this ruffian, who didn't even seem to have noticed him.

He pounded back along the gallery, uncaring what noise he made, and took the next flight of stairs three and four at a time. His blood ran cold when he saw all the half-open doors. The burglars clearly had been along here, looting jewels and money, no doubt, while the guests and their hosts were all busy at the ball.

A well-planned game, then. Not that he cared right now. He burst into his own room, all but skidding to a halt.

At first, he sagged with unspeakable relief, for his wife was not there. Nor was anyone else. But he did not need to turn up the lamp to see that drawers had been pulled out and upended, and that the window stood open. The burglars had certainly been here...

He strode to the window and peered down, but there was nothing to see on the ground. Deep scratches in the paintwork of the sill showed where some kind of hook might have anchored a rope for the ruffians to climb up, or to lower their loot. He heard the distant crunch of feet on gravel, though he could see no one. He turned back into the room, dread warring with hope.

"Eve? Are you hiding? It's only me."

No answer greeted him. But his heart was in his mouth as he opened the wardrobe door and looked under the bed. There was nowhere else for her to hide here.

He strode to the bell pull and tugged it repeatedly. And that was when he noticed the blood on the floor.

Swiping up the lamp, he turned it up and crouched down, his heart beating with fear. It was definitely blood, an alarming little pool of it. *Please God, don't let it be Eve's...*

And then, mercifully, his practical nature took over.

He marched along the passage calling her name, to no response, until he reached the banister, when he leaned over and shouted to the footman below, "Fetch Sir John! The house has been burgled and Lady Wolf is missing!"

He leapt down the stairs, even faster than he had gone up and bolted out of the front door. Snatching up one of the picturesque torches from its wall sconce, he marched around to the ground beneath his bedchamber window.

There were no dents to show where objects had landed—they must have used a cushion of some kind to preserve the stolen goods. But there were several clear footprints in the muddy ground. Two people, he reckoned, had climbed up this way. And come down again. And one set of prints, pointing away from the house, was much deeper than the same set that had approached it.

His blood chilled.

By then, the alarm in the house had clearly been raised, but the thieves had gone.

"What is it?" Sir John asked beside him.

"They've taken my wife," Aidan said bleakly.

"You can't know that," Grandison objected. "She could be anywhere in the house. The servants are already looking, and I've sent for my constables. Come in and—"

"They're getting away," Aidan said impatiently. "Lend me a lantern and a pistol? I'm going to saddle my horse."

# Chapter Ten

With the aid of torch and lanterns, Aidan found only two places from which the burglars had entered and decamped: under the drawing room window where he had seen the stranger, and under his bedchamber window, both being on the darker side of the house, away from the ballroom, the front door, and the kitchens. It had, he thought grimly, been a well-timed and well-planned burglary.

Only, why had they taken Eve? Either she or one of the burglars had clearly been injured, but either way, taking her with them made no sense.

Until he heard the whispers.

Several of the guests had spilled outside to see what was going on, or to beg Aidan to leave pursuit to the constables, while others had fled to their rooms to see what they had lost. Pushing through the outdoor crowd toward the stable, he heard someone murmur. "Someone clearly told the miscreants all about the house and the party. What if she was one of them?"

Aidan stopped dead. Every instinct was to find the man who'd said such a vile thing and knock him to the ground where he belonged.

"Well, she's not one of us," came the response. "No one knows anything about her."

"I do," Aidan said savagely. He had no time for such nonsense. He had to find her. If she was still alive...

Atlas was happy enough to receive him, even in the dark, and with the lantern's help, Aidan found it easy to follow the footsteps of the retreating burglars to the muddy track that ran parallel to the main drive to the gates, half-hidden by tall, gracious beech trees from the drive itself. But once he was through the gates and onto the road, things grew more difficult.

Someone had taken the trouble to wipe out the prints. Aidan rode several yards in each direction and eventually found the clear print of one solitary man, and then one horse heading west. As though one of the burglars had departed later than the others and forgot to disguise the direction of his horse. The man he had seen in the drawing room perhaps.

Or just a passing horseman who had nothing to do with Grand Court. After all, it was impossible to tell when these hoof prints had been made, though they were surely later than the afternoon's rain. Aidan pursued them anyway, since he had no other clue, and was rewarded a hundred yards or so down the road by a larger cluster of hoof prints, as though his man had caught up with the main party and they all travelled onward together.

He was on the right track, but felt no triumph, only grim relief that he was not losing Eve's direction. Probably. All his focus had to be on the tracks and every so often he found them obliterated, whether by accident or design, and had to try both forks in the road and several paths at the crossroads before he picked them up again. They always took lesser roads that avoided villages—and that added to his hope that he was on the right track.

Until they followed a sign to the village of Cresswell. The back of his neck began to prickle with unease. He could not even see the village ahead, although he saw one solitary light on his right. A few yards on, a track led toward it. He paused a moment to listen and peer around him. He could do Eve no good if he was shot or injured in an ambush. Perhaps they knew he was following by now...

His lantern showed him no obvious attackers. But it did show him a sign, half-hidden by a straggly hedge, to the Black Bull. An inn...

He hesitated, for he could see many hoofprints carrying on toward Cresswell, along with wheel tracks and footprints. The path to the inn showed similar chaotic traffic, impossible to differentiate. Eventually, he turned Atlas toward the inn, dismounted in the empty yard, and told Atlas to wait. He generally did.

His heart beating with possibilities, both good and bad, he marched through the door into the light.

A sleepy innkeeper in his night cap with a coat over his night gown sprang to his feet. "Doctor..." He scowled. "Oh. You're not Dr. Ells. Sorry, sir, what can we be doing for you?"

A quick glance had shown Aidan no threatening shadows. There was a light on the stairs leading to the upper floor, and one in the passage leading no doubt to the kitchen. He could hear no voices, but someone moved above the ceiling.

"I'm not sure," Aidan said slowly, gazing at the nightcap. "Have I arrived in the middle of an emergency?"

"Somewhat," said the man. "Got a poor young lady upstairs and the doc—Here! You can't just barge up there!"

Aidan could and did, though it was no doubt unwise. With the innkeeper pounding after him, he took the stairs three at a time and followed the light on the right, spilling under a door.

This door flew open and a large woman in a mobcap exclaimed, "Thank God! Are you the new doctor?"

"No. Is your sick young lady my wife?"

Even in the dim light, the woman's plump cheeks blanched. "Lord love you, I hope not, sir, for she ain't opened her eyes since she was brought here. Come in and see for yourself."

"Seeing being all you'll do," the innkeeper growled behind him, barging into the room almost beside him.

Aidan saw at once that it was Eve.

For one thing, her beautiful, sparkling ballgown, spattered with mud, had been spread over a hard chair. For another, her still, pale face on the white pillow, even without the vitality that was familiar to him, could belong to no one else.

The world tilted and he had to grasp the door to steady himself.

"Is she…?" His voice was hoarse, alien, and he didn't know how long it would last.

"She's breathing, sir. Garrick's sent for Dr. Ells. No need to hang around, Garrick, he's her husband all right. You go and wait for the doctor."

Obediently, the innkeeper departed, and Aidan sank helplessly down on the edge of the bed, taking Eve's cold, lifeless hand in his.

"Poor young lady," Mrs. Garrick said. "What on earth was she doing out in her finery in the middle of the night?"

"I think she was abducted," Aidan said. With sinking stomach, he saw the matted blood in her hair, and the rough, stained dressing upon it.

"I've cleaned it sir, but she must have taken a hard knock. It'll need stitching, I think, but the doctor will know."

"How…how did she get here?"

"Young fellow brought her in and bolted again. Wearing a mask too that made Garrick and me—"

"A mask?" Aidan interrupted, distracted. The man he had seen in the drawing hadn't been masked—had he? "What sort of a mask? Like a loo mask? Or—"

She scowled. "Like a highwayman's mask, and we know they've had a couple of highway robberies over by Beldon, so Garrick was just going to fetch his shotgun, when the young fellow just puts her down on the settle—gentle-like—growls, *Look after her and get her a doctor.* Leaves a gold coin on the table and bolts again! We was outraged, thought she was some thieves' bit of muslin, but not with those hands and certainly not with those diamonds!" She nodded toward the dress on the chair.

*How odd they didn't take the diamonds.* The thought flitted vaguely through his mind, even as Mrs. Garrick said the words.

"Strange him paying for the doctor too," she added. "Expect they don't want to hang for murder. Mind, they'd hang for highway robbery, too."

Aidan was hardly listening. He had his ear close to Eve's pale lips. He felt her breath on his skin, though it was terrifyingly weak.

"That sounds like the doctor now," Mrs. Garrick said, bustling out.

And indeed she came back a moment or two later with a brisk, middle-aged man clutching his medical bag. Reluctantly, peculiarly terrified, Aidan made way for him.

He supposed it was guilt, but the sharp, intense pain constricting his throat and stomach felt like fear. And grief. Could this really be the end of their acquaintance? So short and full of such surprises...

"A nasty wound," the doctor said, glaring at him. "What happened to her?"

"I don't know. I wasn't there. I just followed her."

"Another young man brought her in," Mrs. Garrick confirmed, "highwayman by the look of him, though to be fair he was careful enough of her in our sight. Left a guinea for you too."

The doctor sniffed and reached for his bag. "Needs to be stitched, so perhaps it's best the poor thing's unconscious. How long has she been like this?"

"Must be an hour," said Mrs. Garrick.

"Maybe twice that," Aidan put in. "If she was unconscious when they took her from Grand Court."

"Grand Court?" the doctor said in sharp disbelief, though he didn't look up from his task. At least he burned the needle in the nearest candle flame before using it.

"There was a burglary," Aidan said. "She must have got in their way."

"What's the world coming to?" Mrs. Garrick wondered.

Aidan, numb, let the doctor work in silence. Only after he'd rebandaged the wound did he speak. "Will she live, doctor?"

"I don't know," the doctor replied. "The blow she took could easily have affected her brain. To be frank, I don't like that she has been unconscious so long, but sometimes it's the brain's way of repairing itself. Blows to the head are notoriously unpredictable." He took a small bottle from his bag. "If and when she wakes, give her a couple of drops of this in water —only a couple of drops, mind! And no more than twice in a day. It should help with the pain. I'll call back in the morning to see how she does. What's your name, young man?"

"Wolf," Aidan said, his attention all on his wife.

"Try not to worry, Mr. Wolf. It will not help her. Keep talking to her. It might rouse her. Goodnight, sir."

IT WAS RIDICULOUSLY hard to contemplate life without her. Which was bizarre considering he had not known of her existence a fortnight ago and he could count their conversations on the fingers of one hand. He resented her and all she stood for, found her mad starts like following him to Grand Court annoying. She had a gift for doing and saying the wrong thing and riling him. If he had been granted the barest chance of twelve thousand pounds without her, he would have grabbed it with both hands and run.

And yet he didn't. If she died now, it would, in fact, be the answer to his prayers. So why did the prospect churn him up with fear and guilt and some profound, unrecognizable ache?

Just because they had reached a better understanding during the ball? A hope that perhaps, if they could be friends, all was not lost? Besides which, it was a tragedy that anyone should die so young, and in such a way...

He knew a brief urge to jump back on his horse and go after the bastards who had hurt her, taken her, and abandoned her here. Rather than sitting still at the inn with this unbearable weight upon him, he would be better employed doing something useful...

And yet he could not bring himself to leave her alone. Not for more than a minute or two at any rate. He rose and went to find Garrick the innkeeper, asked him to send a message to Grand Court to say that his wife was injured and that he would stay with her at the Black Bull.

Then he returned to the bedchamber, sat down on the bed, once more taking Eve's hand in his, and rubbing it gently. He imagined she stirred, but her eyes did not open.

"Won't you wake up, Eve?" he said softly. "Please?"

He bent and kissed her fingers and when he raised his head, her eyelids fluttered open. For a moment, pain intensified, for his father had opened his eyes in the moment of his death. But though Eve's eyes were cloudy and a little unfocused, there was surely expression, life.

Gradually, her gaze fixed on his.

He smiled, his relief overwhelming. "There you are."

A frown flickered on her smooth brow, and she winced as if even that tiny movement caused her pain.

"Who are you?" she asked hoarsely.

PAIN HAMMERED IN HER head. As the strange room and the strange man holding her hand emerged through the mists of her vision into the candlelight, she felt more surprised than afraid. Mostly, she wanted her head to stop hurting.

"There you are," he said, as if he knew her.

He had a good face—knee-meltingly handsome. Moreover, his anxious grey eyes were kind and when he smiled, the skin at the corners crinkled. He must smile a lot because those laughter lines were pleasingly deep...

"Who are you?" she asked, not yet worried by his unfamiliarity, just curious.

His eyes widened. "I'm your husband."

The hammer in her head gave an extra-hard blow and instinctively she drew her hand free of his, to reach up and touch the source of the pain. She found a bandage.

"What happened to me?" she asked in surprise.

"I was hoping you could tell me that. You seem to have been abducted during a burglary. At Grand Court."

*What is Grand Court?*

*Why don't I remember something as important as a husband?*

"Your name," she said, struggling, trying to force herself to remember, "is..."

"Aidan," he said after the appalled silence. "Aidan Wolf."

"Then I am—" She broke off as panic surged like a tide. She stared at him, scrabbling in her mind for any familiarity. "*Who am I*?"

"Eve," he said low.

"Eve. Mrs. Wolf." It didn't sound right. Didn't feel right.

"Lady Wolf," he corrected.

It felt no more familiar and no less wrong.

"We are not long married," he said. "Less than a fortnight. Your maiden name is Romilly."

Was it? It meant no more than Wolf.

"Why don't I remember?" she asked hoarsely. "What is wrong with me?"

"You got a nasty bump on the head. The doctor has been and stitched it. He left you this for the pain." He picked up a bottle from the night table. "Let me give you a couple of drops."

"Yes, please," she croaked. Anything to take away the grinding, throbbing pain. Even thinking hurt. She watched him splash a little water from a jug into a cup and add a couple of drops from the bottle.

Propped up on pillows, it was easy to take the cup from him, though she felt weak enough to drop it. She held it in both hands and drank it, eager for it to make everything right again.

He rose from the bed and she panicked that he was about to leave her. Stupid when she didn't even know him. Her husband, dear God...

"I'll send Mrs. Garrick to make you comfortable. She's the innkeeper's wife."

She didn't know Mrs. Garrick either, but apparently they had never met before tonight so that didn't matter so much as forgetting her husband. The woman helped her to the chamber pot, then back into bed, where she bathed her face and hands. By then she was very sleepy and the throbbing of her head had begun to ease.

"Is he...is my husband..." *What strange words.* She swallowed. "Has he gone?"

"Of course not. I'll send him to you."

Although he was a stranger, there was a desperate comfort in his return to the room. She felt able to close her eyes, to give in to the whirling dizziness. When she woke, it would all come back to her and the world would not be so terrifying.

SHE WOKE TO DAYLIGHT. Though her head still hurt, it didn't feel as unbearable. The man from last night sat in a beam of sunlight shining through the bedchamber window. He was sitting at a desk, busily writing. The scratch of his pen across the paper was oddly comforting, considering she still couldn't remember a thing about the man who wielded it. Or about herself.

She reached for the cup of water on the table, and he turned to her at once.

"Eve. How are you?"

"Better, I think." She took a sip. "But I still don't remember anything. How can I not know who I am?"

"It will come back," he said reassuringly. "The doctor may be able to help. Are you hungry?"

"I don't know." Anxiety seemed to be getting in the way.

"Some eggs and toast, perhaps?" he suggested.

Since he had already risen and was halfway to the door, she did not object. And in fact, when a worried-looking maid brought it all in, her stomach rumbled in a most unladylike fashion. She thought he might have heard it, for he smiled.

Oddly, it was almost comfortable breakfasting with him in this way. He sprawled on the bed like a boy on a picnic and they ate scrambled eggs on toast and drank surprisingly good coffee. He amused her with tales of secret midnight feasts with his brother, inevitably discovered by the household adults because they never thought to sweep the crumbs off their beds.

They had almost finished when Dr. Ells arrived. He was no more familiar than anyone else, but at least he was no one she was supposed to know.

"Very glad to find you awake," he said, taking her husband's—Aidan's—place beside her. "You gave us all a bit of a fright. Let me just change this dressing and have a look at the wound..."

"I can't remember anything, doctor," she blurted. "I don't know my own name. I don't even recognize my own husband."

His brows lifted, though he seemed more interested in her wound. "Amnesia. Interesting. I have not come across many such cases where the memory loss lasts for more than a few minutes. But I'm sure everything will come back in time."

"What if it doesn't?" she whispered.

"And what if God strikes us all dead tomorrow? There is no point in worrying about either possibility. Nature will take its course. As God will His. The wound looks fine, considering. Do you have a thundering headache?"

"A nagging one. It thundered last night but Aidan gave me drops..."

"Take them again if it becomes too bad but no more than twice a day until I see you again."

"Till you see her again?" Aidan repeated. "May she not be moved?"

"Where were you thinking of going?"

"My home. Wolverton Hall, some thirty miles from here."

"I would not advise it at this stage. All the jolting would be most uncomfortable for your wife. Resign yourself to a couple more days here at least." Dr. Ells placed a fresh dressing on her wound and bound it in place with quick, deft fingers. "One moment."

He went out quite suddenly, leaving her and Aidan looking at each other in some bemusement, but he was not gone long. He came back with a hand mirror, which he held in front of her face.

She gazed at a stranger. Brown hair, brown eyes, decent, pale skin. She was glad for Aidan's sake that she was not ill-looking, even with a bandage around her head. She was lucky to have him to care for her. And he clearly did.

"I don't know her," she said. "The woman in the glass. She could be anyone."

"Perhaps you remember your mother? Or your father?"

She had not even thought of them. She tried to, then shook her head.

"Your mother is dead," Aidan said, "but your father is very much alive."

"Mr. Romilly," she said, recalling the name Aidan had told her.

"You lived with him until recently. And with your sister, Miranda."

She shook her head.

Dr. Ells lowered the mirror and laid it on the bedside table where she could easily reach it. "Don't force it. The memories will return in their own time. In the meantime, plenty of rest and good food. No strong spirits. If your head does not hurt, you could try sitting in the chair for dinner. Tomorrow, you could go downstairs, with your husband's help, try a little fresh air, but no long walks yet. I'll come back the day after tomorrow. Mr. Wolf, perhaps you'd show me to the front door."

# Chapter Eleven

Though eager to know what the doctor wished to say to him, he also dreaded a disclosure of some deeper injury.

"Your wife's case is unusual," Ells said abruptly as they crossed the inn's empty common room. "I have come across men who forget moments just before and after an accident, but this total amnesia frankly worries me."

"Are you saying she will never get her memories back?"

"I'm saying I have no idea whether she will or not. It would be common sense to encourage her by speaking of your shared past, places and events you have experienced together."

Aidan felt heat seep into his face. "I'm afraid we do not share much past at all. I have known her less than a fortnight."

Ells blinked, pausing with his hand on the front door. He pushed it open. "Yours was a sudden, passionate relationship? Were you happy?"

Aidan looked down his nose at him.

"I don't ask from vulgar curiosity," Ells snapped. "Was she unhappy enough that she might not *wish* to remember?"

"Christ, I hope not."

The doctor scowled at him. "That does not fill me with confidence."

"Nor me," Aidan admitted. "The truth is, ours was a marriage of convenience arranged by her father. I imagine we both resented it. She had an understanding if not an engagement to another man her father disapproved of."

Unthinkable that she could be missing Neville so much that her mind had decided to block her whole life.

He reached up and rubbed the back of his neck. "Would it help or hinder to bring him here? With her father and her sister?"

"It could not hurt if it helped jog her memory."

"I'll send for them today."

He wrote to Romilly at once and was just in time to add his letter to the post bag before the London mail coach galloped in to collect it.

Returning to Eve's room, he found Mrs. Garrick there. She had clearly spread the ballgown over the bed and Eve was fingering it with some awe.

Eve glanced up at him. "Did I really wear this?"

"Yes, you did. It looked very beautiful on you."

"Mrs. Garrick says a highwayman brought me here. Why didn't he steal these? Are they not real diamonds?"

"Oh, I think they are."

"I must be very extravagant. Perhaps the highwayman felt sorry for me."

More likely, he was discouraging pursuit by abandoning her at the Black Bull. Still, he did not seem to have extracted any of the pins.

"I've written to your father and your sister," he said. "And to Mr. Neville."

"Who is Mr. Neville?" she asked, without much interest.

He caught and held her gaze. "The man you wished to marry before your father gave you to me."

Her eyes were serious for a moment and then smiled a little shyly. "Did I mind?"

"I think you did. I'm not sure how much. I found a book in the coffee room—one of Mrs. Radcliffe's novels. Would you like me to read to you?"

"Yes, I would. Thank you!"

"Then you like Mrs. Radcliffe?"

She closed her mouth, frowning, and sighed. "I don't know. Let's see."

Mrs. Garrick bustled off and Eve settled back against the pillows. He read a chapter to her and she seemed utterly enraptured.

"Go on!" she encouraged. "Oh, unless you are tired."

"I'm not, just mindful of the doctor's orders. How is your head?"

"Not so bad. Aidan?"

In what he had begun to think of as their real life, she had never called him his name, always, my lord, or Lord Wolf. He rather liked the sound of it on her lips – informal, almost warm.

"Yes?"

"How long have we been married?"

"About ten days."

"Are we on our wedding journey?"

Fresh heat seeped into his cheeks. "No. To my shame, it did not enter my head."

"Oh." A frown formed and was deliberately banished.

"Ours was a marriage of convenience," he said with rare difficulty.

"Then you did not love me," she stated. "And I loved Mr. Neville?"

"I believe so."

"Were you happy with that? It does not seem very convenient for either of us."

"There were compensations. Your father paid my debts."

She accepted that, nodding slowly. Impulsively, he reached out and took her hand. "We were getting to know each other at the ball. I was content with my bargain."

A distracted smile acknowledged the kindness. "Perhaps I shall sleep now."

She slid down onto the pillows, and he raised the covers up to her shoulders.

"I wrote to Grand Court too," he said, "asking them to send over your things."

"Do I have much?"

"You didn't bring much. You didn't mean to stay but I persuaded you."

Her closing eyes flew wide open. "Why?"

"Oh, to make us more comfortable. Go to sleep now."

*WHOEVER THIS MR. NEVILLE was, I must have been mad to prefer him to Aidan.*

The thought came to her as they played a hilarious game of jackstraws that afternoon. Aidan had found the game in the common room along with Mrs. Radcliffe's novel. They were playing on the bed.

Aidan had a charmingly carefree laugh, and it seemed he brought his complete attention to everything he did. Without cheating for her or against her, he took on every problem as though it was of world importance, then howled with mirth when he caused everything to collapse.

She was sorry when the game ended, but just as they were shovelling the straws back into the box, the little maid Jilly appeared clutching a handful of cutlery and asked if they would like dinner.

"Oh, yes, please," she said brightly. "And Dr. Ells said I could get out of bed for it too."

"I'll set you up at the table," Aidan said, lifting the other chair from the desk and carrying it over to the round table where Jilly was setting two places.

Hastily, Eve smoothed her borrowed nightgown over her legs beneath the covers, and accepted Aidan's help to place the borrowed robe around her. For some reason she blushed as she slid out of bed—perhaps because she looked so ridiculous in Mrs. Garrick's voluminous garments.

But Aidan didn't laugh at her, merely smiled in a conspiratorial sort of way and gave her his arm for the ridiculously short distance. She didn't need to lean on him, but she did, just to make him feel useful.

She rather liked the feeling of being supported, although she hoped uneasily that such poor spirit was not habitual to her.

They were served by Mrs. Garrick and Jilly, who were clearly not used to entertaining the Quality at their inn but did their cheerful best. Eve liked them. And she liked that Aidan did not appear high in the instep either. She had learned that she was not gently born—her father was a mere cotton mill owner with many other strings to his bow—even though she had married a baron. She gathered Aidan was one of those land-rich, money-poor gentlemen.

How did she know about such people when she did not even know her own parents' names?

She was enjoying a small slice of apple tart with fresh cream to finish the meal, when they heard the distinctive arrival of a coach in the yard below.

"Another mail coach?" she guessed. "Or the stage this time?"

"No," Aidan said, rising and crossing to the window. "I rather think... Yes, it's a private carriage. Lady Grandison herself, with a basket and various bags...and Miss Cole."

"Oh dear," she said nervously. "Will they want to see me?"

"They will want to be assured you are well. Lady Grandison is a kind hostess and Miss Cole seemed to be a new friend to you. You might recognize them."

"I might," she agreed, though she doubted it. Why would she recognize social acquaintances when she did not know her own husband? Unless she knew them better than she knew him. Lowering thought.

Aidan went down to meet them and brought the two ladies into the room.

Miss Cole was lively and pretty, Lady Grandison all that was amiable. Both seemed very concerned for her, which was kind. She wished she could recall her friendship with them but she just didn't. They did not make her more uncomfortable by harping on this weakness, merely joined Eve and Aidan in a cup of tea, and told them the latest news about the burglary.

"Sir John is the local magistrate as you know," Lady Grandison said, "and he thinks the burglary is possibly related to the recent highway robberies committed over by Beldon. He's hoping to catch the miscreants before they vanish into the rookeries of London, but he doesn't seem very hopeful. I am quite mortified! My guests have lost jewels and coin, Sir John many family heirlooms, and some of his favourite porcelain and antiquities. And all while we were dancing in the ballroom below, blissfully unaware of the crime being committed over our heads!"

"Don't be mortified, my lady," Aidan said. "You can hardly blame yourself for being burgled! And you may yet get your stolen goods back."

"Lord Wolf is right, ma'am," Miss Cole said. "And if you ask me, now that the danger is over, I think everyone is delighted to be part of such a story. None of it will reflect badly on you." She smiled. "I'm just glad Lord Wolf found you, Eve. He was beside himself with worry."

That was interesting to her, if she could believe it...

"We brought your things," Lady Grandison told her, "as Wolf requested. But my hope is you will be able to return with us to Grand Court."

In truth, she found this idea daunting in the extreme. Not just the inevitable jolting of the journey but being among a houseful of people she could not remember.

"How kind you are, but I don't believe I could just yet," she managed.

"The doctor has forbidden her to travel until he has seen her again," Aidan added.

"Dr. Bagshott?" Lady Grandison demanded.

"No, Dr. Ells."

"Never heard of him. Bagshott is a good man—shall I send him over?"

"Thank you, no," Aidan said firmly. "Or at least, not yet. I think Eve needs rest and peace to recover properly."

She breathed a sigh of relief, although another thought struck her. "If you would like to go back to the party, Aidan, I shall be quite content here with Mrs. Radcliffe for a few days. I shall send word to you if anything changes..."

"No, you won't," Aidan said. "As the man said, *Here I stand.*"

The ladies departed with good wishes, leaving behind a basket of delicacies from Lady Grandison's cook. Jilly put away the clothing they had brought. Eve examined the two morning gowns and a travel dress, together with a pelisse, a bonnet and a travelling cloak, a few shifts and petticoats, a fine lawn nightgown, and a hairbrush. None of them seemed familiar.

"I appear to travel light," she said to Aidan when he returned to the room. By then she was back in bed in her own fine nightgown and looking forward to another chapter of Mrs. Radcliffe.

But as it turned out, she fell asleep only halfway through.

ON THE PREVIOUS NIGHT, Aidan had slept in one of the hard chairs by the bed. Tonight, he helped Jilly make up a truckle bed in Eve's room, very, very quietly, so as not to wake her.

It was silly, really. They were married. There was no reason in the world why they should not share such a large bed. But he had married the Eve who existed before the accident. This Eve, beguilingly similar and yet tantalizingly different, was new to herself as well as to him.

The same chivalry that had made him lie on top of the bed at Grand Court, now kept him out of it altogether at the Black Bull. Even though in many ways he was closer to this Eve who relied on him, than to the previous Eve who had despised him and rightly so, although she had claimed not to during their dance. He wanted to believe that.

Aware that she might well prefer privacy altogether, he still could not bring himself to leave her alone all night. He was too afraid of a relapse.

And yet so soundly did he sleep, waking only to bright daylight, that he doubted he would have heard anything short of a cry for help. As it was, he could hear her now, moving surreptitiously about the room.

Afraid she was ill again, he raised his head and she froze.

She stood beside the big bed, staring at him. One hand clutched her bedcovers, as though she had been about to draw them back and climb back in. The other grasped a bundle of clothing to her bosom. Her hair fell loose about her bare shoulders, for her nightgown without the robe he had seen at Grand Court, was a surprisingly wispy affair of lace and temptation. And it so happened that she stood in a beam of sunlight that shone right through to her delectable, slender figure.

Desire, unexpectedly fierce, surged through his veins. Fortunately, so did humour, for the sight of her standing there so unmoving, as though she still hoped to evade attention, was suddenly funny.

His lips twitched. "Are you cold?"

A blush stained her skin from the neckline of her night rail to the hairline of her forehead. "No," she said, clambering onto the bed and hiding herself beneath the covers. "I meant to dress in bed without your waking."

"Like on a winter morning," he said with a quick grin, remembering boyhood occasions when he had dressed under the warm bedclothes.

She looked bewildered. He doubted she had known many cold mornings and she clearly couldn't remember them if she had.

"I've got a better idea for a more restful start to the day. I'll fetch you coffee from the kitchen, then leave you in peace to dress wherever you like."

"Am I..." A flustered look crossed her face. "Am I a *modest* person?"

Aidan propped up his head on one hand and regarded her. "You would seem to be. Though to be fair, we have not spent much time under the same roof."

The familiar little frown flickered between her brows. "I find that odd. I cannot remember you at all before we met in this room, not your face or your name. And yet somehow, you do not *feel* like a stranger. *I* feel like a stranger."

"You must feel very alone and very frightened," he said gently. "But you are dealing very bravely with the situation. I think that is your character."

"Then I haven't...changed?"

He hesitated from sheer ignorance. "Perhaps you are a little less defensive, but your family would know more—"

"Why was I defensive?" she interrupted. "Did I not like you?"

"I gave you no reason to like me," he said ruefully.

"But you do now," she said. "I must always have liked you."

"I wish that were true." The words slipped out with a crooked smile, but he found he meant them. And that was not so much to do with regret for past behaviour as with the odd intimacy of the moment. A waking conversation with a friend that he had never known in his adulthood.

She *liked* him. That pleased him right down to his suddenly restless toes.

"Then if you are still feeling modest," he said, "avert your eyes while I find some clothes. I'm afraid I am stark naked again."

She averted her face somewhat hastily and he was sure she blushed. "Then you are *not* modest?" she asked.

"Just thoughtless," he said, sitting on the side of the bed and reaching for the clothes he had cast on the floor beside it last night.

He pulled on his pantaloons and was fastening them when she moved very slightly. She was watching him. He bent for his shirt and rose to pull it on, hoping she was not disgusted.

"This has happened before," she blurted.

The shirt fell around him as he spun to face her. "You are remembering?"

She stared at him, concentrating hard, then blinked and blushed again, shaking her head. "No. But *something* was familiar."

"Grand Court is full of guests. We shared a bedchamber. Perhaps you are starting to remember."

He tucked his shirt into his pantaloons and left her, wondering at the odd conflict in his mind. He wanted her to be whole in mind and body. She *needed* to remember. Only...only he rather liked things as they were, without all the baggage of what had gone before.

Then he remembered dancing with her. What had gone before was not all bad either. Brushing the confusion aside, he clattered downstairs to beg coffee from Mrs. Garrick who was in the kitchen, sharply instructing a sobbing Jilly to pull herself together before she scalded herself.

"Is something wrong?" he asked, and they both spun on him in surprise.

"Lord, no, sir, just my girl being soft. What can we do for you?"

"Coffee, if you please. And my wife is feeling well enough to come downstairs for breakfast."

He waited in the common room for his coffee, giving Eve time to make herself comfortable in private. He was not much used to considering others, so it was a novel sensation.

IT WAS A DAY OF PLEASANT discoveries. After enjoying coffee sitting on his wife's bed with her, he visited his horse and then took himself for a brisk walk, both to ease his cramped, restless limbs which were unused to being cooped up for so long, and to give Eve time alone. Although happy to look after her, he didn't want to irk her.

He returned to find her outside in the paddock behind the stables, one arm around Jilly, the maid who was no longer weeping.

"Kitten died," Garrick said disgustedly, coming up behind him. "Jilly broke her heart for it—it'd lost its mother too soon and Jilly cared for it almost from birth. But it was never right and couldn't survive. Never saw such a fuss over such a tiny creature."

"Have you buried it?" Aidan asked, with vague memories of losing an old, beloved hound when he was about ten years old.

"Your lady wife took her to say a prayer over the little thing. Made our Jilly easier."

Aidan had felt better too when he and the old kennel master had buried his dog with ceremony. There weren't many, he reflected, who would have bestirred themselves for a tavern maid's grief. He was proud of his Eve, although the kindness all came from her nature and was nothing to do with him.

Garrick was shaking his head. "Never understood females," he muttered. "But if the girl stops snivelling, I'm grateful."

Eve's outing into the fresh air appeared to do her no harm. Over breakfast in the common room, they talked about animals and the possibility that she had owned one, then about Aidan's love of horses. Afterward, he took Eve to meet Atlas in the stables and she stroked his nose and gave him an apple, which the horse consumed with great speed.

"I wonder if I ride?" she said.

"If you don't, I can teach you at Wolverton Hall."

She accepted that and they took a short stroll, talking of everything and nothing.

It was some hours later, during a game of chess—Garrick had uncovered an old board with most of a set of pieces—that Aidan realized he was not merely content but actively happy. Spending time in a country inn getting to know a fascinating girl he was not even bedding.

"What are you smiling at?" she asked suspiciously. "Am I in check and haven't noticed?"

"No, you're far too downy for that. I was just thinking how much I like you."

She flushed with clear pleasure, although she laughed it off. "What, just because I can play chess? Or do you imagine you'll win if you distract me with flattery?"

In fact, the honours were even. They were setting up a third game to decide the issue when a post-chaise came clattering into the inn yard, and he saw Romilly alight ahead of his daughter Miranda, her aunt, and a stranger he took a moment to recognize as the clergyman who had married him to Eve. Mr. Neville, Eve's former betrothed. The man she had loved. And Aidan had laughed when she'd told him—not from malice, merely from somewhat unsympathetic humour.

A surprisingly powerful jolt of jealousy shot through him. Neville was a good man who cared for orphans. Aidan could not compete with that.

But this was not about Aidan. It was about Eve's recovery. On impulse, he said nothing about the new arrivals, and all Eve's concentration was on screwing up a fresh scrap of paper to act as the missing white pawn.

Romilly all but burst into the house, calling loudly for the innkeeper. Eve glanced up, taking in the whole party before they even noticed her, and turned back to the board. She moved the papery pawn forward two squares. Aidan met it head-on.

"Eve!" Miranda squealed, rushing across the room to them.

Aidan rose, his attention all on his wife who looked merely startled.

"Look, Papa!" Miranda cried, pointing an accusing finger at Eve. "There's nothing wrong with her! It's all a hum!"

"Naughty puss," said the aunt indulgently and yet with an irritated look in her eyes. "I daresay she brought us here just so we could meet some of his lordship's noble friends."

Eve's startlement had turned to bewildered alarm. He could see no trace of familiarity or even recognition in her face as her gaze jerked from person to person. She stumbled to her feet, trying to fix a pleasant smile to her lips. She did not turn to Aidan for help, but he could not leave her struggling.

He stepped round beside her, letting his fingers brush hers in comfort. "You must excuse Eve's reticence. I'm afraid she still remembers nothing of her previous life before the injury to her head."

"What injury?" Miranda said scornfully.

But Romilly was scowling. His hand shot out, sweeping back the hair that Aidan had arranged to hide the bandage around Eve's forehead.

They all stared at her. Eve stared back, clearly feeling she was in the wrong but unaware how to fix it.

Aidan closed his fingers around hers. "Eve, this is your father, Mr. Romilly, your aunt, Mrs. Strang, and your sister, Miss Miranda."

While they all gawped at each other, Aidan turned his attention to the silent clergyman who stood behind the family, looking both serious and uncomfortable.

With odd reluctance, Aidan reached between Romilly and Miranda, his hand held out commandingly. Neville grasped it instinctively.

"A pleasure to see you again," Aidan said, drawing him nearer. "Though I could wish it were in better circumstances. Eve, Mr. Neville, the old friend of yours who married us."

Eve blinked at him. Her eyes, which had seemed to be feverishly searching her family's faces, now looked blank with disbelief.

"Mr. Neville runs the charity for your orphans," Aidan said.

"Orphans?" she said, vaguely.

"Good grief," Miranda said in mingled awe and disgust. "Is Eve mad?"

# Chapter Twelve

In fact, Eve was wondering the same thing, though for entirely different reasons. She had, apparently, preferred this rather ordinary, middle-aged man to *Aidan*.

With a growing sense of unreality, she took in Mr. Neville's gentle, worn and worried face—the face of a good, hard-working man she could never look down upon. It was not even a matter of comparing it to Aidan's handsome countenance. Though she could not actually remember any of them, she knew there were many handsome men in the world. It was Aidan's urgency for life, the vital blaze of his eyes, the sheer humour and joy of constantly changing thoughts and expressions that was lacking in Mr. Neville. There was no spark.

And yet she would have married him rather than the beautiful, fascinating man beside her. Even now she could *feel* that spark, burning into her fingers, spreading through her veins into some kind of unstoppable conflagration.

*Love. Of course I love Aidan. So...*

She smiled a little tentatively. "Forgive me. I'm afraid I don't yet recall anything or anyone."

Miranda, the rather lovely young woman who was her sister, sniffed. "You remember *him* well enough, though, don't you?" She jerked her head at Aidan.

"I know who he is," Eve said. "But no, I don't remember him from before the accident."

"What happened?" Mr. Romilly demanded, glaring at Aidan as though he were to blame.

"We don't quite know," Aidan said calmly, "but it happened during a large scale burglary at Grand Court when Eve was abducted, possibly for the jewels in her ballgown."

Miranda's jaw dropped. "Jewels in her gown? *Eve*?"

This confused Eve, since the jewels in the ballgown were the only evident thing she knew of herself. She clung to Aidan's comforting fingers, anchoring herself.

Fortunately, Garrick bustled up, talking of rooms and dinners and the strangers moved away with him and his wife, everyone talking at once.

"I rather think our peace is over," Eve murmured ruefully.

"Is nothing familiar about any of them at all?" Aidan asked.

She shook her head. "They confuse me even more."

His arm came around her shoulders in a quick, brief hug that made her heart beat faster. "I'm sorry. I thought they would help."

She smiled up at him. "I expect they will in time."

Still, she could not help regretting the loss of their solitude. She felt weighed down by the need to justify herself to her family, even to Mr. Neville, whereas Aidan just let her be. And the flowering of their knowledge of each other was precious to her. Clearly there had been difficulties between them before, resentments and quarrels caused largely by their reasons for marrying in the first place. His debts, her rich father's social ambitions, the thwarting of her own marriage plans.

To Mr. Neville.

*Inconceivable.*

They dined early again, this time in company with Eve's unfamiliar family.

Miranda came downstairs complaining that she had to share a bedchamber with her aunt. Her disgust increased when she realized they were not the only people dining in the common room.

"What a nasty little house!" she said, shuddering. "Are there no private parlours to be had, my lord?"

"I'm afraid not. This is a small house and there is very limited space."

Miranda brightened suddenly. "I have a brilliant notion! Why do we not repair to Grand Court? If Lady Grandison invited you to return..."

"She has no room for all of us," Aidan said firmly. "And in any case, we await the doctor's permission for Eve to travel."

"She looks fine to me," Miranda muttered.

"Why does she want to go to Grand Court?" Eve murmured to Aidan when she could.

"To meet marriageable gentlemen," he whispered back. "Preferably a duke, though a mere earl is the highest ranking nobleman present there, and he is betrothed to Harriet Cole..."

Eve nodded her understanding. It was vaguely funny, but she wondered if she too had been such a blatant climber. If so, it would certainly explain Aidan's reluctance to marry her. She wondered if she had been close to her sister, for she did not much like her now. She did not much like any of them—except possibly Mr. Neville—which she knew to be undutiful and made her feel guilty. The thing was, she had the odd sense they did not much like her. They were not here to care for her so much as to make use of her. Behind their smiles and complaints and watchful eyes, she sensed they were plotting.

After dinner, they all pronounced themselves exhausted by their journey from London and retired early.

"Mrs. Radcliffe?" Aidan suggested. "Or a short walk?"

"The walk first," she decided. Her head, which had merely ached in a mild, nagging kind of way throughout the day, had begun to hurt more sharply again during dinner, and she thought the fresh air would do her good.

They strolled in companionable silence through the inn yard and along the short gravel drive to the main road. As her headache began to ease, she realized how aware she was of the man at her side, the feel of his strong arm under her fingers, the quick, restless grace of his movements, the clean, masculine scent of him among the fresh, night smells of the countryside.

She said abruptly, "Can I ask you something?"

"Yes?"

"Who did you give up to marry me?"

His glance was so plainly surprised that it was a relief. "No one. Why should you imagine there was?"

"I don't know. It just popped into my head when I met Mr. Neville. I think you must be a popular man and no stranger to women. You like me well enough to look after me now, yet you resented marrying me for the money."

He grimaced. "It is how marriages of convenience work. I always knew I would have to marry money in the end, for the sake of my family and the land, but I always imagined it would be a time and a lady of my own choosing. I resented the whole situation, the debts, my own pride...but mostly I was angry about the trickery."

Her eyes widened. "My father tricked you?"

He shook his head. "I think he did, a little, but as you pointed out, that was my fault. I did not read the agreement properly before I signed it. I underestimated him and overestimated him at the same time."

"Was I complicit?" she asked, frowning.

"No, I think it was as big a surprise to you as to me. And of course, you had Mr. Neville, though your father disapproved." His gaze remained on her face. "Did it hurt you to see him again?"

She sighed. "It baffled me. He is a good man but he is not a...a *romantic* man."

He smiled. "Neither am I."

"Mrs. Radcliffe would agree with me that you are. Are you truly not in love with anyone else?"

"I don't think I understood love. Women were a pleasure to me, a treat, like the best of foods and wines and games all rolled into one. Not the living, breathing, maddening, *human* reality. Not one of them was truly part of my life."

Her heart hammered away in her breast. She said, "I...I want you to know that even though I can't remember anything, I am content with our marriage. I would like to be part of your life. You are all of mine."

He stopped beneath the spreading branches of the inn's apple tree that grew over the fence. The light from the moon showed her the wonder in his eyes, a sort of surprised tenderness. His hand came up and touched her cheek.

"You are too sweet and too kind. And I am trying very hard not to take advantage of you. Of your vulnerability. Between us, your father and I took away the choices that were your right. I want you to choose from knowledge."

"How very chivalrous of you," she said shakily.

His lips twitched. "I thought so."

But his gaze was on her mouth, and her own dropped without permission to his. Greatly daring, she stood on tiptoe and kissed his lips, a quick, shy salute that made his breath catch in surprise and her own vanish altogether.

His hand moved, cupping her cheek while his thumb touched the corner of her mouth. He bent his head and kissed her back, a soft, tender caress that melted her bones with sweetness. And then his mouth fastened with more purpose and invaded.

She clutched him for support, her arms sliding up around his neck, while he held her to his strong hard body and the kiss went on and on and—

From nowhere, it seemed, she saw another vision of Aidan with a woman who was not her, though they were kissing just like this. The picture flitted through her mind and vanished before she could grasp it. But as though he felt her withdrawal, he raised his head.

"Forgive me. You are too sweet, and I'm afraid it's my impatient nature to move too fast."

"I kissed you first," she whispered, and he smiled.

"I'm so glad you did. Allow me more kisses, only not now when you have made me weak."

"You don't seem weak."

"Trust me, I am falling."

She didn't quite know what he meant by that, but at least when he turned them back toward the inn and drew her hand back to the crook of his elbow, he kept her close to him.

She said, "I remembered something. Another kiss."

"I never kissed you before tonight. I expect it was Neville," he added, tightening his lips.

"It was you. But not me."

He glanced at her frowning.

She shook her head. "I don't know where it came from. Imagination, probably. It just felt real, only I can't make it lead anywhere else."

"That might be a good thing. Though it leads me to hope you might have been jealous."

"Of whom?"

"Of anyone," he said vaguely. "A little hot chocolate and Mrs. Radcliffe?"

"Perfect."

"WELL!" DR. ELLS, THOROUGHLY searching her face when he called the following morning, actually smiled. "You are looking much better."

"I feel very well," Eve said cheerfully. She was up and dressed already, having enjoyed another companionable night in the same room as her husband. Her husband who had kissed her... She had fallen asleep recalling every moment of that kiss, and every word of the conversation surrounding it. It made her very happy and excited, as did their every interaction since. Trying to keep her wayward mind on what the doctor needed to know, she added, "And my head barely hurts at all, unless I touch it."

"I'll take a quick look at it." He reached down to unwind the bandage. "Do I gather your memory has returned?"

"No, not yet."

He must have heard something in her voice because he cast a sharp glance at her face while he worked.

"It no longer troubles me so much," she explained. "I can be happy in the present."

"You have your family here now. That must make you feel more comfortable."

"Not really," she said honestly. "It is my husband who comforts me." She hoped she wasn't blushing.

"Is it?" the doctor said. "He led me to believe you were not close before your accident."

"It is strange how things work out."

"This is healing well," the doctor pronounced. "No corruption. Any signs of fever?"

"None."

"Good." He placed a fresh dressing on her wound and wound the bandage back around her head to hold it in place. Then he stood looking down at her. "Don't fight the memories, Mrs. Wolf—I beg your pardon, *Lady* Wolf. Life is not a fairytale with just one happy-ever-after."

"I'm not fighting against them," she assured him. "In fact, there was a moment yesterday evening when I did recall something—or thought I did—but it was like a flash I could not relate to anything else."

"To do with the accident?"

"No, I don't think so. Am I well enough to travel now, doctor?"

"I would not like you to be jolted all over the country. Unless you are very uncomfortable here, I would stay put for another few days."

"Thank you." In truth she was relieved, for although the presence of her family had disrupted her guilty comfort somewhat, she had a notion that going home—to Aidan's home —would end their growing closeness. They would have separate bedrooms, probably, and separate lives.

She wondered again if they had ever been intimate. Had there been a wedding night, a consummation? And how was it her mind knew of such impersonal things as the ways of the world? Things she must have been taught, such as how to read and write. The Bible. Shakespeare. Even Mrs. Radcliffe. History. Pieces of music. Right and wrong. Love. And yet she could not recall her own name, her homes, the people in her life.

The doctor looked at her, his expression faintly troubled, for a few moments more. He seemed about to speak, then merely inclined his head and picked up his bag.

"Good morning, Lady Wolf."

AIDAN HAD DELIBERATELY left his wife alone with the doctor this time, aware that there were intimate matters she might well wish to discuss. He was very aware he had done nothing to earn the warmth of her closeness, that it was to some degree false, a clinging to some anchor in what must be a very frightening, dark sea.

He should never have kissed her, of course. Not until she could recall her true feelings, at least. She had just been so sweet and tempting...and utterly desirable. He had never been so moved by a mere kiss.

How odd, when he had barely brought himself to look at her before. He hadn't even known she was beautiful when he'd married her. He had noticed her outward placidity hid strength of character and unexpected spirit, but she really was a completely delightful companion. Quick of wit and humour, thoughtful, warm, compassionate, so...Eve. She was unique, and he had only just begun to realize it.

And now he started to fear the return of her memory when she would remember the true Aidan.

Ruefully, he clattered downstairs in search of more coffee—it was raining outside and a walk was unappealing—and discovered the common room empty save for Mr. Neville tucking into breakfast. He nodded to the clergyman in response to his civil "Good morning," and wandered into the kitchen.

Mrs. Garrick shooed him out again, though at least with the requested coffee.

Neville half-rose from his seat again. "Join me, my lord?"

Aidan did not wish to join him. But curiosity as to the nature of this man's relationship with his wife got the better of him. He sat down opposite him.

"I did not get the chance yesterday to thank you," Neville said. "For allowing your property to be used for our orphans."

"I'd forgotten all about it," Aidan said truthfully. "The building is no use to me, and it's better housing someone. My wife felt strongly about it."

Neville's gaze dropped to his plate once more.

Aidan watched him. "I'm told I stepped on your toes."

"I beg your pardon?"

"Marrying Eve. She told me you had an understanding."

"It was a pleasant but impractical dream," Neville said. "Her father would never have permitted it."

"She is of age," Aidan pointed out.

Neville shovelled a large forkful of bacon into his mouth.

"Why didn't you fight for her?" Aidan asked.

Neville had to finish chewing before he could answer. He took his time, but seeing that Aidan wasn't going to go away, he appeared to give in.

"Miss Romilly—Lady Wolf—is a remarkable young lady. I think... I didn't believe that it would ever quite happen. I never understood why she looked at me."

*Neither do I.* "You are a good man," he said aloud. A man who would fight for his cause, his orphans, but not for his own personal happiness. Or Eve's. With sudden insight, Aidan realized she would have been too much for Neville, too full of ideas and energy, eclipsing him, wearing him down. Eve would never have thought that. But Neville had. The man might miss her, but part of him was relieved.

*I would fight for her. To my last breath.*

# Chapter Thirteen

The knowledge stunned him, so much so that he could neither laugh it off nor shove it out of his mind.

Eve came downstairs with Dr. Ells, who seemed satisfied with her progress and merely left instructions for her continued rest and peace. Aidan repeated those instructions pointedly to her family when they joined everyone for breakfast.

"But what on earth are we to *do* here for *days*?" Miranda demanded.

"Talk to Eve?" Aidan suggested. "Remind her of her past life with you, family events, secrets you shared."

Miranda looked doubtful.

"I have a business to run," Romilly muttered. "I cannot sit around doing nothing."

"You may post back to London when you choose," Aidan said. "Neville here has duties too. He is already booked on the mail coach, though I suspect he'll be a trifle squashed."

Neville did indeed depart on the mail coach. Eve did not appear to miss him.

"You could post back to London with Aunt," Miranda said to her father. "I could stay to look after Eve."

Eve did not look outwardly alarmed by this threat, though Aidan felt her body tense beside him.

"Don't worry," he murmured when the family had all trooped back upstairs. "I think she still imagines going to Grand Court with you. Dolt and Fool would be all over her like twin rashes."

She smiled. "Who the devil are Dolt and Fool?"

"Dolton and Poole. Gazetted fortune hunters due to their gaming habits."

"Like you," she said, frowning.

He shifted uncomfortably. "Not quite. I think the rain has gone off. Shall we risk a stroll in the mud?"

She agreed readily enough, and he went upstairs to fetch her cloak and bonnet.

Their room was already occupied, not by Jilly making the beds but by Miranda, gazing with awe into the wardrobe.

"They're my pins!" she said in outrage, grabbing at the ballgown. "Eve took them!"

"They were hers to take," Aidan pointed out. "Can I be of service, Miss Romilly?"

"Not unless you know where she's hidden the rest of her clothes. I was looking to see if I could borrow something, should we go to Grand Court, for I have nothing very suitable with me. As for the diamond pins, they were as good as mine. Eve never used them."

"As you see, she did, if not with their intended purpose. And the rest of my wife's clothing is at Wolverton Hall. We shall not be returning to Grand Court."

She turned to him, irritated and yet scornful. "Have you forgotten the terms of your twelve thousand pounds, my lord? You are to do your best for me too."

"The best thing anyone could do for you is teach you some sense. Better born females than you have been ruined for considerably less than lurking in gentlemen's bedchambers."

"My sister's bedchamber!" she blustered, though colour had swept into her cheeks.

When he merely continued to gaze at her, she flounced. "Don't pretend you wouldn't rather have had *me* to wife than boring old Eve. When I'm a duchess, I'll ruin you both if I choose with just one word!"

"With manners like those," Aidan said, "my best efforts couldn't win you a pig farmer. Good morning, Miss Romilly."

The door slammed behind her, leaving him concerned not for her threats but for Eve's past. No wonder she had been willing to marry him just to get out from under the same roof as her sister.

Clearly, the best thing he could do for Eve right now, was to get rid of the family he had so naively summoned for her good.

RETURNING FROM THEIR walk, Aidan found a hand-delivered note from Sir John Grandison awaiting him. Apparently some of the stolen goods from the burglary had been recovered some distance away, abandoned, apparently, when the gang dispersed with several constables in hot pursuit. Grandison had requested the aid of the famous Bow Street Runners to run them to earth.

Aidan read his message in the common room while Eve went upstairs. He frowned over it for a bit. He had been so concerned for his wife and then consumed by the new feelings flowering between them that he had barely thought of the thieves.

"Not more bad news, is it, sir?" Mrs. Garrick said, pausing in her sweeping to gaze at him.

"Oh, no. It's quite good, I suppose. The law is closing in on the burglars, and some of the stolen items have been recovered already. The runners are after them now."

"I don't suppose they'll be long finding that young chap who brought her ladyship here then."

"Probably not. But why pick on him? At least he brought my wife here where she could get help." Though why he had taken her in the first place was another mystery.

Mrs. Garrick shrugged. "I just mean he should be easy to recognize."

"Well, I suppose the mask would stand out," Aidan said sardonically, "though it hardly proves the features beneath."

"A mask don't hide a man that lame," Mrs. Garrick said with some satisfaction. "Nor the blood on his coat, neither."

Aidan blinked. "You never said he was lame."

"You never asked. I daresay I also never mentioned he spoke well for a gent of the high toby."

"Are you saying he was a *gentleman*?" Aidan asked in disbelief. A gentleman who limped, a not-quite stranger he had bumped into at the Grand Inn...

"Not saying that, sir!" Mrs. Garrick said in shocked tones. "Stands to reason he ain't a *real* gentleman! But he fair dragged that left leg and he weren't rough in his speech."

And quite suddenly the man glimpsed at the inn on the day of the ball stood vividly in his mind's eye. So did a gentleman making his difficult way through a very different, much more crowded and riotous inn on the night of the prize fight. A friend of Snake Sanderly who had played dice with them...

"That's where I saw him before!" he exclaimed. "I'll bet you anything it's the same fellow. I need to see Snake."

"YOU'RE GOING TO RIDE over to Grand Court?" Eve said, quickly hiding her reasonless dismay.

"Not today," Aidan replied, searching beneath the truckle bed for the worn copy of Mrs. Radcliffe. "I thought if I left first thing, I could be back before your family annoys you too much. By then I should have found a way to send them politely on their way."

He came up triumphantly with the book held aloft.

"You don't want them here after all?" she said.

He seemed to hesitate. Then he said carefully, "I'm not sure you and your sister were ever friends."

*We weren't.* How did she know that? That Miranda always made her feel bad? Plain, charmless, unloved... A few different moments flashed through her mind, confrontations, demands, tears, sitting alone at parties watching Miranda dance and flirt.

*I liked to dance...*

*I danced with* him!

The force of the memory seemed to spin her away from him. But she didn't see the lightening sky nor the familiar inn yard below, she saw the woman Aidan had been kissing. And she knew her name.

*Mrs. Archer.* And she was at Grand Court, where Aidan wanted to go.

Fear for her new happiness caused her legs to buckle and she sat down abruptly in the window seat. Aidan was talking but she was too consumed by the returning memories, unveiling like a curtain drawing back.

And she remembered that she was used to this, to smiling and hiding.

It didn't come all at once.

But she had lost the moment to tell him immediately and the more that came to her, the more she feared.

He *liked* her as she was here, now. So did she. She didn't want the old baggage. It hurt more than her head ever had. Because he had married her for his brother's debts. For twelve thousand pounds and a dowry. And he escaped immediately to Grand Court rather than be under the same roof as her. No wonder he had been so angry when she followed him there.

She could not concentrate on Mrs. Radcliffe, nor on chess or even jackstraws. She contributed little to conversation, which no one seemed to notice but Aidan, who insisted she go early to bed and rest.

She didn't think she would sleep, so churned up was she by memory and pain. But she did. And when she woke, she was herself again. Old Eve had combined with new, and they were not so very different.

Except that the new Eve was loved and happy and that was the version she wanted to keep. The Eve who longed to make Aidan happy.

Perhaps she never intended to hide the truth from him forever. But she was actually glad he meant to go early to Grand Court. The truth surrounding her accident was still a blur. She could not recall how she had got from the Grand Court ball to the inn. And she really didn't want to talk about the memories that *had* returned. To do so would surely lose her his precious care and attention.

"HOW ARE YOU THIS MORNING?" Aidan asked, on discovering her eyes were open. He sat down on the side of the bed.

"Much better," she said, smiling. "I was suddenly exhausted last night. I shall be more careful today."

"I should be back before dinner time." He hesitated. "Don't pay too much attention to Miranda. Sisterly rivalry has made her spiteful."

"She can't hurt me."

He touched her pale, soft cheek. "I did marry you for money. But every marriage begins somewhere. It is the present that counts."

Her smile turned a little tremulous. "I know. I am grateful to Patrick and his ten thousand pound debt. Take care on the road. You don't want to run into those highwaymen-cum-burglars."

"Oh, they are long gone." He bent and kissed her forehead. "Go back to sleep if you can. Get Jilly to help you dress."

"I will."

Rather touchingly, she dragged his hand to her lips and kissed it. And suddenly he didn't want to leave.

Forcing himself, he did.

Atlas was glad of the exercise and pounded happily across the miles to Grand Court. The ground wasn't too wet and they made good time, arriving at Grand Court in time for breakfast.

Leaving Atlas in the stables with instructions for his feeding and rest, Aiden strode into the house and caused squeals of apparent joy in the breakfast parlour.

"Wolf!"

"My lord!"

"Tell us all! How is your poor lady?"

The last came from Lady Grandison, who rose to meet him.

Aidan bowed over her hand. "My lady does much better, thank you. She sends her gratitude for all the good wishes—and for your cook's treats. The doctor advises quiet for another few days, but I rode over to see how things are here and to have a word with Sir John if possible." He looked around the table, nodding amiably. "And you, Snake."

Sanderly raised his eyebrows. It was satisfying, not to say amusing, to see Snake, who normally eschewed morning company, dancing attendance on his betrothed at breakfast.

"Sir John will be down directly," Lady Grandison said. "Fetch yourself a plate and join us until then!"

Having worked up an appetite on his ride, Aidan was quite happy to break his fast in company. He heard that a few of the other guests had left the party already, too unnerved by the shock of the burglary. The rest, most of whom had returned to the ballroom the night of the burglary to finish their dance, had no intention of changing their plans.

"I do admire you, Lady G," Helena Archer drawled from across the table. "You take everything in your stride—guests arriving without invitation, others departing without a word, or returning unannounced, burglary..."

"No one can say your parties are not interesting," Aidan said, grinning at her ladyship. "I'll expect pirates at the very least for the next one."

"You can host the pirates," Lady Grandison retorted. "Now that you have a hostess, we expect to be entertained at Wolverton Hall."

"You may be sure of an invitation," he said.

Grandison had not made his appearance by the time Aidan had eaten his fill, so he wandered outside to wait for him. Happily, Snake followed him into the garden.

"While we're private," Snake said, "a friendly warning in your ear."

"About what?" Aidan asked without much interest.

"During the ball, just before the burglary was discovered, Helena Archer enticed me out of the ballroom and into one of the unlit rooms upstairs, on the pretence that Harriet needed my help. When I got there, Alicia Eldridge awaited me. I walked straight back out again and on the ballroom stairs encountered Helena once more with Harriet, apparently bringing her to me. Harriet was perfectly well. Does any of this sound familiar to you?"

Aidan scratched his head. It did ring a bell in his mind, although so much had happened since that he had to dig about for it.

He shrugged. "Between ourselves, Mrs. Eldridge came to me, enticing me outside, where Helena awaited me to say an apparently fond farewell. Are you saying they were playing some reciprocal game to spite you and me and our respective ladies?"

"It crossed my mind. Before my experience, I did happen to see Alicia with Lady Wolf which I thought odd."

Aidan frowned. "Are you saying Alicia intended to take my wife to witness my fond farewell to Helena?"

"I'm saying she might well have done so. Your wife left the ballroom and went to her bedchamber in the middle of the ball."

"She had no reason to be there," Aidan said slowly. "I thought that at the time. You think Eve saw me?" Helena's kiss had certainly been extravagant and hardly chaste.

"If there was something to see, I imagine she did."

"I'm almost grateful she lost her memory," Aidan said with suppressed savagery. "Did you confront either of them with this?"

"No, for I—being notoriously discourteous—merely abandoned them both without explanation."

Aidan sighed. "Everything has consequences."

Snake gazed straight ahead. "Harriet likes your lady. She thinks you should consider what you have there."

"She is right. I have been slow and self-absorbed if not plain stupid. I hope you are going to marry Miss Cole."

"I am," Snake said cooly. "Here's Grandison."

Their host took them back inside to his study and closed the door, saying, "What's it all about, Wolf? Has your lady remembered more about the burglary or her abduction?"

"No, but I have. I recalled it after Mrs. Garrick—at the Black Bull—gave me a fuller description of the man who carried my wife into the inn and left her there. A tall, fair young man with a limp." Aidan glanced at Snake. "Sound familiar?"

"Not offhand," Sanderly said.

"I saw such a man at the Grand Inn here," Aidan said. "I was in a hurry so I didn't pay him much attention at the time, but it was on the day of the ball and he looked dashed familiar. I just couldn't think where I'd seen him before. It was your friend, Snake, from the Duck and Spoon. You remember, the night of the prize fight? We played dice."

Sanderly stared at him. "I remember the fight and the dice and Captain Berry."

"That was his name!"

Snake's lip curled. "Are you accusing an officer and a gentleman, badly wounded in the service of King and country, of abducting and injuring your wife?"

Sanderly could be damned unpleasant when he wanted to be, but unlike most of Society, Aidan had never been afraid of him.

"I'm saying it's damned suspicious. What was this Berry doing at the Grand Inn? You didn't know he was there, did you?"

"Perhaps not," Grandison intervened, "but we invited no one called Berry, and no strangers were admitted to the house."

"Apart from a gang of burglars," Aidan said dryly.

"So Berry is a burglar too?" Sanderly stood up. "I've heard enough. And if you go around slandering a good man, Wolf, I'll knock your teeth out. Good morning."

Aidan jumped to his feet, grabbing Snake's arm as he turned to the door. "No, wait, Snake, who *is* this fellow? I'm willing to believe I'm wrong—convince me."

"I don't need to," Snake said, brushing off Aidan's hand somehow without touching him. He could be the haughtiest creature alive when he chose to be.

"You said he was a hero at Salamanca," Aidan pursued. "Invalided out, presumably. Who is his family? How does he live?"

"His father is a clergyman. I have never inquired into his financial circumstances any more than I have into yours."

One didn't, of course, as a gentleman, but Aidan couldn't let it go. "Where was he going when we met him at the Duck and Spoon? Where, incidentally, we spoke quite openly about the Grand Court party."

"I hope you know a good dentist."

Grandison intervened. "Gentlemen, let us not be hasty. At the moment there is nothing to prove this Captain Berry was the man who delivered Lady Wolf to the inn. We do not even know how he came to be in her company. But whoever he was, he wore a mask, and that is suspicious. I will inquire at the Grand Inn about this fellow that Wolf saw and what he was doing in the neighbourhood. It does seem quite a leap to link the two men, but until we actually catch any of the gang, we won't know."

Sanderly merely curled his lip and opened the door.

"I know he's a friend of yours, Snake," Aidan said. "So am I."

Sanderly turned his head quickly, betraying surprise. The man had few friends, mostly through his own fault. Aidan had never believed the whispers against him of cowardice and treachery.

"People have reasons," Aidan added ruefully, "for all sorts of bizarre behaviour. I should know."

A frown tugged at Snake's brow, and then he went out without a word.

"He defends this fellow as he never defended himself," Grandison remarked.

"No one else ever defended Sanderly either," Wolf said.

"I suppose he never seemed to care."

*He cared*, Wolf thought.

"I'll look into the fellow," Grandison said, scribbling something on the paper in front of him. "Berry, is it? What's his Christian name?"

Aidan rummaged in his erratic memory. "Jonathan," he said triumphantly. "Of the 95th Rifles."

Grandison wrote that down too, then replaced his pen in its stand and fixed Aidan with a slightly awkward-looking gaze. "Are you staying?"

"Oh no, thank you. I'll go back to the Black Bull just as soon as Atlas is rested enough to carry me."

"You should know," Grandison said reluctantly, "that more unpleasant rumours have started up since the burglary."

"What kind of rumours? They're not blaming *that* on Sanderly too?"

"Not on Sanderly, no. But I'm afraid there are whispers against your wife."

"My wife?" Aidan repeated, uncomprehending, before he recalled the words he'd overheard when he rode out of Grand Court in search of her.

*"Someone clearly told the miscreants all about the house and the party. What if she was one of them?"*

*"Well, she's not one of us. No one knows anything about her."*

A flush of anger swept up from his toes, burning into his face. "How dare they? Because she was not born into their class they assume she is a criminal? She of all of us here has no need of more money!"

"It makes no sense," Grandison agreed at once. "They are happy enough to say you married her for her money. The inconsistency of her risking hanging to acquire more does not appear to weigh with them."

"Small-minded fools," Aidan said furiously. "Who is saying such things?"

Grandison threw up one hand. "Consider my position as host of this party. There has been enough scandal here without you rampaging about the house bloodying noses and demanding satisfaction. All I will say is, you are charging a stranger with similar crimes with just as little evidence."

"But that's..." His impetuous denial tailed off as the words sank in. He cast Grandison a rueful glance. "You think I was wrong to bring this Berry up?"

Grandison shrugged. "It is never wrong to supply information. I would—and have—investigated other strangers passing through the area, as well as local people being where they had no real business to be."

A breath of cold air touched him. "Including my wife being in her bedchamber during the ball."

"And being in the masked man's company to be carried to the inn. Why did he not steal the diamonds from her gown?"

"She cannot tell us!"

"Because she has lost her memory. Some have called that convenient."

Fresh fury threatened to erupt in Aidan. He half-sprang up from his chair and then fell back into it as, from nowhere, Eve's own words, spoken just before he left the Black Bull, forced themselves into his mind.

*"I am grateful to Patrick."*

He had been saying the initial reasons for their marriage no longer mattered. He had told her he had married her for the money to pay his debts. He had never told her that the debt was Patrick's. *How did she know?*

On her own wishes, she had never allowed herself to be alone with her family since their arrival at the Black Bull. She had not heard it from them. The only solution was that she remembered.

His ears sang. Was her memory loss total deceit? For the "convenience" Grandison spoke of?

*Have I been gulled?*

Only when it began to slip away did he realize the intensity of his happiness during the last few days, of his unacknowledged new hopes of companionship and love, of the strength of the feeling which might have begun without his noticing at Grand Court, but had bloomed so quickly and so fiercely at the inn.

It could not all be lies.

Could it?

# Chapter Fourteen

Eve had been aware of her slip almost as soon as she made it. Fortunately, Aidan did not appear to notice and went away with that same achingly tender look in his eyes.

She could almost believe she had won him. Somehow. That together they would be strong enough to face anything.

*I have lied to him*, she thought, stricken. *I can never take that back.*

And yet, was it not worth it to hold onto his love? To make him happy and comfortable?

She remembered his cold distance in the carriage from London to Wolverton Hall. His fury when she had dared to appear as his wife at Grand Court. Their many lesser quarrels and the contempt in his eyes that amounted to hatred. She compared all of that with his kindness at the Black Bull. Last night he had flirted, kissed her, acknowledged they had a new beginning that he wanted.

Without her defensive gruffness, her deliberate masking of true feelings, she must be more appealing. How could she go back now to being his indifferent, contemptuous wife? Not that she ever had been. She was just even more hopelessly devoted now.

Only hunger drove her downstairs for breakfast, which she took with her family.

"I must say it's a bit much of Wolf to bolt off to Grand Court," Papa complained. "He knows I need to return to Town."

"You must feel free to go, sir," Eve said. "I no longer need careful watching and, in any case, he will back by dinner time."

Miranda laughed shrilly. "Is that what he told you? I'll bet you anything his mistress is there."

"Miranda!" Aunt exclaimed in shock, while Papa glared with rare annoyance at his younger daughter. "You cannot speak of such things."

*What mistress?* She hoped she had not asked the question aloud. For one thing, she already knew the answer, didn't she? She had seen him in Helena Archer's arms. She further suspected Helena's friend had urged her there to witness the unbearable sight, just to remind her of her powerlessness as a despised wife.

Miranda was trying to complete the job. No doubt she had come off worse in some encounter with Aidan—his warning about her surely confirmed that—and she was stirring the pot for revenge. Miranda had always hated not to be first or best and her spite could be vicious.

"I understand you still need his help for your own social ambitions," Eve said now. "I would not try to humiliate him if I were you."

"*You* couldn't humiliate a potato, even in your right mind," Miranda retorted.

"I fail to see why I would even try. But I shall give you a word of advice. You may think you are pretty enough and captivating enough to say what you like in any society. In his world, you are not. You will excuse me, Papa? Aunt? I'm going for a walk."

But Miranda had the last word.

"You think he loves you," she said in tones of stunned disbelief. "Because he's hung around you from guilt, trying to look after you! Look at yourself, Evie. He's not coming back tonight or any night. Why should he?"

"Miranda!" Papa snapped. "Must you be so confoundedly vulgar?"

It seemed she must. Ignoring their father's interruption, she continued triumphantly, "Not when Helena Archer is at Grand Court."

Eve kept walking but her knees felt as shaky as they did when she first woke after the accident. Miranda read the scandal sheets. She and therefore the world knew the name of Lord Wolf's mistress.

AIDAN'S HEAD WAS STILL spinning with conjecture and fears and denials, when the Grandison groom brought Altas out to him, fed, rested, and re-saddled. He barely noticed at first that Snake Sanderly walked out of the stables behind them, until he realized the earl was going to walk past without speaking.

"Snake?" Aidan said. "Grandison will inquire about him. He's also inquiring about my wife, so don't take it personally."

Snake paused and turned fully to face him. "I suppose one is as likely as the other. He must be desperate."

Encouraged, Aidan said, "I know the feeling. Any ideas how to be rid of social-climbing in-laws? Particularly a pretty young thing desperate to be a duchess."

"As it happens, I did sight a duke over by the Duck and Spoon when we stayed there."

"I don't recall any dukes at the fight. Which one?"

"The Duke of Death, naturally. He didn't take the London or Harwich roads or the route to Grand Court. He might have been going to Southend-on-Sea. For the sea bathing."

Wolf laughed. "Never met his grace but I hope for his sake he's strong-willed." He swung himself up into the saddle and walked the horse the few paces to Sanderly, who looked surprised when he bent to offer his hand.

After only the smallest hesitation, Sanderly took it in a brief clasp and strolled away.

For Snake's good, as well as his own, Aidan hoped this Captain Berry was not involved. He could not imagine how Eve would even have come in contact with such a man. Had the unlikely Neville merely been a cover for Eve to meet a suitor even less pleasing to her father? Was Eve helping him out of love? Or ignorance?

Or was there no connection between them at all? Grandison was right. He had no proof that the masked man was Captain Berry. He certainly had no proof that his wife lied to him, except in the matter of her memory, but even that might have been a mere glimmer of its return. She might remember more and more each day without consciously noticing...

As he rode, he argued with himself, castigated himself as alternately gullible and idiotic. But when he thought about Eve, from first impressions to last, he found he just could not believe in her guilt. She was undoubtedly sweet natured and kind. Her shy awkwardness might have vanished with her memories, showing the delightful person she had always been, but that was not deception.

When Aidan stirred himself, he was perceptive. And deep down, he knew Eve. Their closeness was no lie, no cynical seduction. She was Eve, not this contorted fantasy Grandison's accusations had conjured. Half-accusations. Grandison did not believe them either. Malicious gossipmongers like Archer and Wriggley, and probably Helena herself, were no doubt responsible.

His troubles began to fall away as Atlas ate up the miles back to the Black Bull. He even began to smile because he was so eager to see his wife again. To talk to her and make everything right between them. To love her.

He clattered into the yard and walked Atlas over to the stables where he handed him over to the ostler. He was just turning away when some movement caught the corner of his eye.

A man emerged from behind the large oak tree. He was tall and fair, wearing a rather disreputable looking coat, and he limped badly on his left leg. Even so, he moved with surprising speed toward the back entrance to the inn's tap room.

HER FAMILY SHOWED NO signs of imminent departure. Eve felt obliged to spend time with them in the inn's common room, where her father wrote letters very busily, Aunt sewed, and Miranda complained.

Eve tried to concentrate on Mrs. Radcliffe's exciting novel, but it was not nearly so much fun without Aidan.

She set it aside when her family dispersed to their own rooms and wandered restlessly toward the chess table. Aidan should be back soon. If he was coming. She prayed he was, for she had made up her mind.

For something to do, she set up the pieces on each side of the board, including the screwed up scrap of paper to act as the missing white pawn. She thought she heard the clatter of a horse's hooves in the yard and her heart began to beat faster. *Aidan? Please be Aidan...*

She tried not to watch the front door, instead moving pieces about the chess board as though playing a real game. Still no one entered by the front door, though when she finally glanced up, she saw someone entering from the left side, from the short passage that led to the tap room.

He did not look surprised to see her, merely stood perfectly still, gazing at her.

Eve could not have moved if she'd tried. For she knew this man. She remembered him perfectly, for she had seen him without the mask in some blurry moment of half-consciousness, and then with perfect clarity before the horse beneath them jolted her back into agony and the returning relief of blackness.

"You're alive," he said, his tone pleased.

"It's you," she said stupidly. "Did you hit me?"

"God, no." He came toward her, and she jumped to her feet, ready to flee. He stopped at once, holding up both hands encased in rough gloves, palms outward. "I won't hurt you. One of my idiots did that and decided to bring you along. Opinions vary as to whether the motive was a doctor or the diamonds on your gown. I apologize for him from the bottom—"

The front door crashed open and Aidan burst inside, hurling himself between Eve and the stranger.

"Aidan!" With joy, she rushed to his side, clasping his arm in both hands.

"You," the stranger said in startled accents.

"Captain Berry," Aidan said coldly.

"Hush, for God's sake, you'll get me hanged."

"I'll do it myself if you harmed a hair on her head."

"One of my oafs thumped her and then thought it a good idea to bring her along. This was the best I could do. She would have died if she'd stayed with us. To be fair, she might have died at Grand Court waiting to be found. Now that I know she is well, I can flee with a clear conscience."

"You've just admitted burglary and part of the assault on my wife!"

"I explained to the lady as a gentleman. As the miscreant burglar, I bid you good day."

With a grin, he actually bowed and strolled away to the front door. Aidan started purposefully after him, but Eve hung onto his arm.

"No, let him be, Aidan. He isn't a bad man, I would swear it. He really did come to make sure I was well."

Aidan swung on her, glaring, his eyes fierce and turbulent with emotions she could not even begin to read. And then he seized her, and his mouth was on hers in the kind of savage kiss she had never even imagined, and instead of being frightened, she let out a gasp of pure joy, threw both arms around his neck, and kissed him back.

"Dear God, Eve," he muttered against her lips. "I was so afraid for you! I don't know what I feared most, that he'd kill you or..." His mouth latched to hers again.

"Or what?" she asked breathlessly, when she could speak.

He groaned. "I have so much to tell you of my own doubts and fears and idiocy. But I believed in you utterly, do you hear? I *knew* you were not in league with him. If you'd loved him, I truly believe I would have killed him."

"Goodness," Eve said, awed and rather reprehensibly more pleased than shocked. "Of course I was never in league with him, but I did remember him as soon as I laid eyes on him, and oh, Aidan, I have to tell you I remembered *nearly* everything before you left but I was so afraid to tell you in case it ruined..."

He tilted up her face as she seemed inclined to look down in shame. "In case it ruined what?"

"Love," she whispered. "I hoped you might love me. Because I always loved you. Even before we married."

His breath caught. "Thank God. I thought you'd despise me again when you remembered."

Her mingled tears and laughter were lost in his mouth as he began to dance her gently across the room to the stairs, passed an open-mouthed Jilly, and up to their bedchamber.

"Tell me to wait, wife of my heart," he said, as they fell against the closed door. He buried his face in her hair—still careful to avoid her wound.

"For what?" she asked bewildered. His heart thundered against her and his body pressed to hers was excitingly hard and wonderful.

It was presumably clear she had no desire to wait for anything, for instead of loving her with mere words, he took her to bed. And there, he showed her the astoundingly physical reality of passion and pleasure. Amid sighs of pleasure, and gasped, tender words, he made her his wife in truth.

IT WAS TWO HOURS LATER before, somewhat languidly, they descended the stairs once more. Her family was already dining. Aidan, buoyed up with the sheer pleasure and the joy of true tenderness he had found in his wife, felt ready for anything.

"You're late," snapped Romilly.

"On the contrary, you are early," Aidan said, holding a chair for Eve. "I thank you for looking after my wife today, especially when I know you are anxious to return to London."

"*He* might be," Miranda muttered. "I'm not. Anyone who's anyone has left Town. And there's nothing wrong with Eve. She remembers everything so you could easily take me to Grand Court with you."

"Oh there's no one worthy of you there," Aidan said, taking his own place next to Eve. "The guests are departing. But I did hear of a certain duke gracing Southend on Sea with his presence."

"Southend?" Miranda said in disbelief. "What does he want there?"

"Sea-bathing is good for the health," Aidan said vaguely. "I don't know his grace personally, so I can't introduce you, but I'm sure a clever girl like you could contrive a meeting. You could try the sea-bathing yourself. For your temper," he added pleasantly.

No one noticed.

"Papa, we must go immediately!" Miranda commanded.

Romilly sighed. "You and your aunt go. The provinces are so damned exhausting."

Eve's eyes danced as they met Aidan's. He had bought them some peace until they could go home and begin their truly married life. And he looked forward to that more than anything ever.

**The ESCAPE Series**

Escape of the Scoundrel
Escape of the Bridegroom
Escape of the Highwayman

**About the Author**

Mary Lancaster is a USA Today bestselling author of award winning historical romance and historical fiction. She lives in Scotland with her husband, one of three grown-up kids, and a small dog with a big personality.

Her first literary love was historical fiction, a genre which she relishes mixing up with romance and adventure in her own writing. Several of her novels feature actual historical characters as diverse as Hungarian revolutionaries, medieval English outlaws, and a family of eternally rebellious royal Scots. To say nothing of Vlad the Impaler.

More recently, she has enjoyed writing light, fun Regency romances, with occasional forays into the Victorian era. With its slight change of emphasis, *Petteril's Thief*, was her first Regency-set historical mystery.

CONNECT WITH MARY ON-line – she loves to hear from readers:

Email Mary: Mary@MaryLancaster.com

Website: http://www.MaryLancaster.com

Newsletter sign-up: https://www.MaryLancaster.com/Newsletter

Facebook: https://www.facebook.com/mary.lancaster.1656

Facebook Author Page: https://www.facebook.com/MaryLancasterNovelist/

Bookbub: https://www.bookbub.com/profile/mary-lancaster

X: @MaryLancNovels https://x.com/MaryLancNovels

Bluesky: @MaryLancaster.bsky.social

TikTok: https://www.tiktok.com/@mary.lancaster1

Printed in Dunstable, United Kingdom

66112582R00099